EMPTY WARDROBES

EMPTY WARDROBES

MARIA JUDITE DE CARVALHO

Translated from Portuguese by
MARGARET JULL COSTA

Introduction by
KATE ZAMBRENO

TWO LINES
PRESS

Originally published as *Os armários vazios*
© Heir of Maria Judite de Carvalho
Translation © 2021 by Margaret Jull Costa

Two Lines Press
582 Market Street, Suite 700, San Francisco, CA 94104
www.twolinespress.com

ISBN: 978-1-949641-21-9
Ebook ISBN: 978-1-949641-22-6

Cover design by Gabriele Wilson
Cover art by John Stezaker: *Mother Night*, 1989, Collage, 27 x 20 cm
© John Stezaker; Photo: Damian Griffiths
Courtesy of Galerie Gisela Capitain, Cologne, and The Approach, London
Typeset by Jessica Sevey

Printed in the United States of America

Library of Congress Cataloging-in-Publication Data

Names: Carvalho, Maria Judite de, author. | Costa, Margaret Jull,
translator. Title: Empty wardrobes / Maria Judite de Carvalho; translated
from Portuguese by Margaret Jull Costa. Other titles: Os armários vazios.
English. Description: San Francisco, CA: Two Lines Press, [2021] |
Translation of: Os armários vazios | Identifiers: LCCN 2021015289 (print) |
LCCN 2021015290 (ebook) | ISBN 9781949641219 (trade paperback) |
ISBN 9781949641226 (ebook) Subjects: LCSH: Patriarchy--Fiction.
Classification: LCC PQ9265.A77 A813 2021 (print) |
LCC PQ9265.A77 (ebook) | DDC 869.3/42--dc23
LC record available at https://lccn.loc.gov/2021015289
LC ebook record available at https://lccn.loc.gov/2021015290

1 3 5 7 9 10 8 6 4 2

This project is supported in part by an award from the National
Endowment for the Arts. This book is also supported within the scope of
the Open Call for Translation of Literary Works by the Luso-American
Development Foundation and funded by the DGLAB/Culture and the
Camões, IP – Portugal.

INTRODUCTION

by Kate Zambreno

My grandmother collected perfume bottles, a seeming whimsy for a woman of such plainness and ferocity. I have three of them, given to me when she was still alive. They lived in a drawer and then later, in a decorative moment, on the bookshelf, where I have since placed them higher and higher out of reach, as my daughter has attempted to climb up to play with them, a slow-moving game between us, until now they are so high up as to be out of view. I tend not to be sentimental about objects, but I at least don't want them to break, this being all I possess from my grandmother, anything else guarded by her surviving daughter, who, having remained unmarried, still lives alone in the house in which she was born, that being the way in my family. The bottles are candy-colored glass—blue and purple twins with matching Bakelite flowers as the stoppers, and another newer, smaller one, with complementary hand-painted purple flowers with blueish-green stems and yellow pistils at the centers, and with a gold atomizer. They are not valuable—objects in my family become antiques only through accruing dust in the house they've inhabited, on mantles and in glass. I can still see the menagerie that resided on the heavy wooden dresser in my grandmother's bedroom, which was covered with plastic and underneath it a lace doily. On top of the doily, viewable through the plastic, were black-and-white photographs: portraits of relatives, baby photos, and photographs of her late husband, who died when she was still a young woman with a young child still at home, leaving her a widow until her death in her nineties, half-paralyzed from a stroke but still ruling the world from her dining room table, waving her grabber at her grown children, gleefully threatening to hit them with it for whatever crime committed, usually (her word) stupidity. The table itself was covered always with at least a cheap cloth-backed vinyl or plastic decorative tablecloth of garish pattern, frayed or cracking at the edges, and for holidays, a nicer solid-colored linen cloth on top. Underneath was the heavy mahogany table, like all the furniture in my grandmother's house, the immovable furniture of generations. My grandmother's collection of perfume bottles crowded next to her jewelry, which was minimal and rotely worn, including not only her heavy wedding band, which my sister keeps asking for, but also her silver watch, which my grandmother must have had to wear to keep time while working the linens counter at Marshall Field's all those decades after becoming a widow, having had to close up her husband's butcher shop and store where she had previously presided behind the register, the calves widening from girlish into matronly, all those varicose vein decades, after suddenly becoming a single mother with a young child to raise, her older grown sons, the twins, away in the Navy, later returning in order to gather around their mother, one staying unmarried and in that house until his untimely death, the other moving away, but not too far, that other being my father, who accrued his own museum, having lived for his own decades in the state of the widower, although his savings account was never the subject of existential dread, he having been the one who made all the money in his marital life, my mother at home with the children, as was the way. She was a saint, an angel, both my uncle, my grand-mother's son, and my father, my grandmother's other son, said about both their mother and my mother, respectively, at their funerals, one having died of an astonishing old age, and the other, at a sudden and tragic middle age. I didn't recognize who they were talking about. All I recognized was the empty monologue of Catholicism, which serves to erase by anointing the woman at home, who only exists in service to others but not to herself. Does she even exist, I often have won-dered, to herself? Writing this I have no idea why my grandmother collected perfume bottles, were they gifts that her sons brought home from over-seas, and they began to unthinkingly accumulate, over birthdays and Christmases? My grandmother cut her ridged nails with the kitchen scissors, she never wore makeup, let alone perfume. I have no idea what my grandmother, or my aunt, or my mother, thought about at night in their empty houses, in the solitude of caretakers. I have no idea if they were unhappy, whether they thought of their girlhood, or when the children were young, whether they had regrets, and if they could, what would they confess? I have no idea because I never asked, and they would never have said. It would have been an impossibility. Their inner monologue would have been closed to me.

What you need to understand is how a woman can become a piece of furniture. The kind of woman who lives in a house like a museum, filled with artifacts of her past relevance. In the great Portuguese writer Maria Judite de Carvalho's only novel, the compact, merciless tragedy *Empty Wardrobes*, published originally in 1966, the widow Dora Rosário manages an antique shop referred to by her young daughter as "The Museum," an occupation secured for her by a pitying network of female acquaintances, the plight of necessary supplications that Carvalho mocks, that bitter sharpness of waking up to a society's cruelty, masked by exhaustion. What you need to understand about Dora Rosário is she is meant to be ancient, past her prime, meaning in the tradition of great women's melodrama, she is thirty-six years old. While he was alive, her incompetent husband refused to let her work, she was supposed to be at home, taking care of her child, who grows to be a cheerfully callous teenager over the course of her mother's decade-long career as a widow. For that past decade as well Dora has lived amid the antique furniture at the Museum, dressing like an "off-duty nun," tending also to her late husband's memory, the required dissolution of self like an ecstasy of sustained mourning brought to an art form. The permutations of her consciousness are an exercise in the way the imagination can drift in tedium, resembling the clerk Bernardo Soares in another famous translation from Portuguese by Margaret Jull Costa, Fernando Pessoa's *Book of Disquiet*. The exquisite style of the passages set amid these baroque objects that possess more value than the solid and unmoving woman hired to guard over them. The ache of this emptiness and dustiness, the matron as a museum:

> She had spent the best part of the last ten years there, among tables large and small, some semicircular and propped against the wall, others like long-legged birds, half-asleep and slightly unsteady on their feet, others standing imperiously on sturdy legs with strong metal claws gripping the floor. There were also sundry writing desks and a tall, delicate Etienne Avril escritoire, chests dating from various centuries, a

solitary Regency lounge chair, its upholstery wearing thin, and many other pieces
of furniture, all with very full curriculum
vitae and all devoured by generations of
energetic woodworms, but still very solid,
gathered together like decaying aristocrats in a home for superior elderly folk.
Glass domes covering beautiful clocks that
had long since stopped, images from the
eighteenth century, ornate boxes, exquisite, elegant ivory figurines, odd plates
held together with metal brackets, a fine
Persian rug, and, scattered here and there
on the walls, frozen after many years in
flight, were a profusion of Baroque angels,
chubby and cheerful, modestly veiled or
else fully clothed and even wearing boots,
all of them with their bird wings spread.
It was there in the Museum—because it
really was more museum than shop, since
it had more visitors than buyers—that
Dora spent her days.

There is a gesture among the elders in my family
of a slight turning away when anything taboo is
brought up, the subjects one is not supposed to

refer to—adultery, divorce, the great unhappiness of a traditional marriage. *Empty Wardrobes* is set amid a cloister of three generations of women who also have been refusing to hear any such taboos, or perhaps truths, except in the quiet hangover of the monologue of a maiden aunt becoming undone (explained away as eccentricities, or an episode), which then catalyzes the midnight confession of the mother-in-law/matriarch—whose aging appearance across the novel is rendered in a series of hilarious grotesques—to her daughter-in-law, Dora, the closed and severely unfashionable widow. This speaking of the unspeakable between generations of women unleashes a series of events, which opens up an abyss of regret for our heroine's wasted life, and, temporarily, a return to the self, or a new self, with optimism's ephemerality and artifice. Then sometime later on, supplying the novel's frame, Dora Rosário, out of will and despair, tells of the tragedy of her life to the devastatingly witty yet still mournful narrator, a former friend and tossed-aside mistress of one of the men, a buffoon, all of the male characters in the book being buffoons, mere shadowy catalysts who still unfairly hold all the power. There is also the teenage daughter, unthinking in her own youth and beauty about her pronouncements of her mother's hopelessness, who never sees her mother's lifetime sacrifice, although there is a recursive sense of her future fate once she gets what she thinks she always wanted, which is to become a rich man's wife.

Reading *Empty Wardrobes* I thought of the great modernist novels of wives, which are by their occupation works of tedium and duration—*The Passion According to G.H.* by fellow midcentury writer of Portuguese Clarice Lispector, Marguerite Duras's *The Ravishing of Lol Stein*, and of course, Virginia Woolf's *Mrs. Dalloway* (although Carvalho's characters are funnier and more cruel than Woolf's). Reading this novel, I felt awakened by the possibility of literature, which is to tell of a consciousness that in real life is rendered dull and redundant, incapable of imagination or higher thought (the disappearance of the clerk, as well as the wife and her past tense, the widow). It feels shocking for such a complete and alive work of literature like this to have been untranslated for so long. This is a hilarious and devastating novel of a traditional Catholic widow's consciousness, encased like ambered resin in the ambient cruelty of patriarchy, an oppression even more severe in the God, Fatherland, and Family authoritarianism of the Salazar regime in Portugal. A work like this, set in the regime of a dictator who weaponized Catholicism and "family values," is by its very nature deeply political, even if (no, *especially if*) it's set in a series of interiors, in the domestic space, in the space of service. I read this novel with something resembling a rapturous grief, as if I couldn't believe this consciousness had finally been rendered in literature, the consciousness of so many women familiar yet unknowable, no longer muted, not saturated with sanctimony but alive, alive with rage transmuting disdain into hilarity by sheer force, alive with intense paroxysms of sadness.

EMPTY WARDROBES

J'ai conservé de faux trésors dans des armoires vides.

—Paul Éluard

It was a spring day which, apparently at least, began and ended like any other spring day: that is what she would have said or, more likely, thought, because she was always a woman of few words. She never said more than was strictly necessary—the bare indispensable minimum—or else she would begin to say only what was necessary, then quickly grow tired, or stop mid-stream, as though she suddenly realized that it wasn't worth going on and was a waste of effort. She would sit quite still then, her face a blank, like someone poised on the edge of an ellipsis or standing hesitantly at the sea's edge in winter, and at such moments, all the light would go out of her eyes as if absorbed by a piece of blotting paper; for all I know, she may still be like that, because I never saw her again. For a long time, I failed to understand that those lapses into unconsciousness,

which is what they were, invariably led her back
to the same place, or, rather, to the same person,
to the same tarnished image of that person, because she was not a woman given to confessions,
as I said. Words were of no use to her in explaining her thoughts, in polishing or disguising
them, which is what most of us do. She would
use them, and then only as a last resort, to say
something urgent (I'm referring, of course, to
the time before the party her daughter, Lisa, gave
for her friends. After that, it would be another
story). And when she absolutely had to speak,
she would fall silent immediately afterward (or,
as I said earlier, stop halfway), and it wasn't only
the light in her eyes that then switched off, for
her body would also droop slightly, as if someone had turned off the power—which, however
low-voltage, at least kept it active—as if her
body had forgotten its original upright posture.
When this happened, she wasn't really there,
although no one knew where she was or who
she was with. In fact, such a thought probably
wouldn't occur to anyone, because her face be-
trayed none of this, only her eyes and her hands,
but who would notice her eyes or indeed her
hands, which lay half-open on her lap, like shells

washed up on the beach? Sometimes when I was with her, I thought that perhaps what she needed was a good shake or, better still, an X-ray, so we could see if she did actually have more inside her than just lungs and a digestive system.

She didn't speak much in the shop either. And she wasn't particularly nice to the succession of employees who worked for her. She knew this and knew, too, that the blame, if there was any blame, lay squarely with her and no one else. She always found it hard to make the first move when approaching other people, regardless of whether they were her superiors or her inferiors. She found it embarrassing. It's true that in the past she had made many such first moves, but they had been necessary, even vital. If she hadn't, what would have become of the two of them, mother and daughter? That's why she hadn't hesitated then, not even allowing herself the briefest of hesitations, however much it pained her.

She did talk to me about all this once, but I think she only did so in order to justify herself, and perhaps her daughter too, a little. She was someone who cared what others might think, especially what I might think. Those ten years of voluntary and involuntary solitude (because she had, after all, chosen a solitude that already existed in the form of grief), had greatly contributed to this. She and Lisa were on one side, and all the others were on the other side. The *others* were the enemy from whom she could expect nothing good, only evil. For her, the *others* continued to be her husband's boss, who was never in when she called ("Senhor Black has just left. No, he won't be back today"; "Senhor Black is out. No, I don't know when he'll be back"), their friends, almost all of whom had vanished (whatever became of them?), his work colleagues (the few who had, gladly or reluctantly, once been of some help), her well-off mother-in-law ("Come to the house and bring the little one, we can feed five as easily as three. But as for money, you can forget about that.").

Money. A word she heard everywhere, all the time, even when she was asleep. People, the *others*, would start making excuses before she had so much as opened her mouth; she only had to turn up in a threadbare coat, with runs in her stockings, untidy hair. The *others* would immediately launch into their excuses, before she had begun to explain the problem, the reason why she had come: "You've no idea how bad things have been lately, a real nightmare. Actually, all things considered, your husband was lucky not to see the state the business is in now, it's a complete mess. I was saying as much to some friends only yesterday: Duarte Rosário was lucky in a way, what with all the people who've been fired lately, he might well have been shown the door himself." There were some who took their wallet out the moment they saw her, and did so slightly aggressively, with a weary lift of the eyebrows, not noticing the rush of blood to her cheeks or her tremulous lips. The fifty *escudo* note would burn her hand even before she touched it, but she always accepted it eagerly, how could she not? Lisa was seven years old and needed to eat well and have iron injections for her anemia. The handing over of the note was always followed by the same words of warning: "I can't keep doing this, you know. If I could, I would. Duarte and me were very good friends. Your husband was one of the few truly decent men I've ever met, possibly the only one. The fact is, though, that everything seems to have gone wrong for me lately. To top it off, my wife has to have an operation." And when it wasn't the wife, it was the son, and when it wasn't a medical emergency, it was a financial one, not just painful but disastrous.

Meanwhile, she would take the fifty escudo note, and in kind, courtesanly fashion, express her regret at their misfortune—and heaven knows how this must have pained her—but as soon as there was a brief pause, she would say: "I absolutely must find a job. Do you know of anything? If you do hear of something…"

The face before her would immediately open in a smile, because, quite unwittingly, she had given the ex-colleague a neat way of bringing the conversation to a close. The man would get up, still smiling: "If I do, I'll let you know at once, don't you worry. Do you still have the same phone number?"

"No, the phone was cut off two weeks ago."

"Oh, dear," the man would say. This was a further obstacle, but not insurmountable. He'd bound gaily over it. "No problem. I'll drop you a line as soon as I hear of something. I assume it's the same address?" he would ask somewhat warily.

"Yes, the same address."

"Excellent, excellent."

They would be standing opposite each other, with a secretary between them. And the man would always accompany her to the door, smiling broadly, as if his sensitive heart had been filled by a great wave of hope, a hope that would surely prevail. Some struck a more realistic note, rather than speaking in purely abstract terms. "What skills do you have to offer?" She would list them (there weren't many), and they would shake their head, beginning to succumb to hopelessness. "It won't be easy, Dora Rosário. French would be useful, and German, of course." She would withdraw into herself then, almost shrivel up if I can put it like that. Since she hadn't learned either of those barbarous tongues, what was she to do? Then there were the more determined ones, who were always full of suggestions. Why didn't she check out the job ads in the newspaper? Why didn't she teach? Teaching was a good job for a woman. But teach what, when she'd forgotten everything? Besides, she had a terrible memory for things that didn't interest her, and she hadn't even been particularly interested in the subject she did end up studying.

Then there were those from whom she would have expected only understanding and friendship, but who had gradually or suddenly gone over to the enemy camp. Friends she had inherited from her mother, friends who were blood relatives or (a few) that she'd acquired by chance over the years. They had kept her company, they had attempted to break the barrier of her silences and her lapses. "Frankly, your husband... I mean, no savings, no life insurance, how is that possible? Men. Selfish to the core, even the best of them. And you with a young daughter too, goodness me..."

She would sob a little, wipe her eyes, sink briefly into the maternal arms of grief, momentarily lower her guard, feel slightly soppy and sorry for herself; then she'd suddenly stiffen, every vertebra alive, and her dull eyes would take on that uncomfortable, over-the-top brightness that made them look like creatures with a life of their own, ready to pounce, to bite, to tear the enemy to pieces. "Duarte did all he could for us, and I won't have anyone saying otherwise," she would say almost fiercely.

The inherited or acquired friend would not return, and Dora Rosário knew this perfectly well. Another corpse, she would think with a shrug; yet another to add to all the others piled in her mass grave. Most of them committed hara-kiri using their own particular methods, but

with others she was the one to deliver the coup
de grâce. A relief? she wondered. Yes, why not?
And she shut herself away still more inside herself, her daughter, and the memory of her husband. She only left the house to ask for a loan, to
look for work, or to convince the baker or the
grocer to let her postpone paying her bills for a
little while longer.

Then, one day, out of the blue, she found an
excellent job. Her only remaining friend from
the good times (everything is relative, but those
past times, had, for her, been the good times),
that friend—who had hovered between her and
the *others* in a kind of no-man's-land, now here
now there, never daring to make too deep an in-
cursion into either territory—had turned up one
day looking all excited, and pretty much handed
her the job on a plate. A relative or friend of
hers, of Gabriela's, owned an antique shop and
was moving abroad, indeed, was obliged to do
so. That man had asked Gabriela if she knew
of some competent person—it could even be a
woman, as long as she was energetic and totally
reliable, of course—who could take over running
the shop. He would pay her well. He was, so to
speak, caught between a rock and a hard place.

Gabriela had told him that she knew just the person, a friend who had recently been widowed, the sort who has lost all interest in life. This man was even now waiting to meet her, Dora Rosário, at number such-and-such on such-and-such a street. "Go on, get going, put your coat on," Gabriela had said. "No, wait a moment, take mine, it's black too." She had sat Dora down, combed her hair, made her change her stockings, and lent her a box calf handbag bought in Paris at Henry à la Pensée. "It's important to make a good impression."

"But I don't know anything about business, Gabriela. Or about antiques. I hate them in fact. They frighten me. They make me feel uncomfortable."

"You'll learn. When you receive your first paycheck, you can buy a few books and read up about it. You're not stupid, you'll soon get the hang of it. And don't say anything to him about that, all right?"

And so it was. She got the job, bought the books, and she did learn, earning enough money over the subsequent years to send her daughter to a school for rich kids as well as to ballet school. Later, she hired an English tutor and a German tutor, who came to the house on alternate days, and all this happened under the simultaneously suspicious and reticent eye of her mother-in-law, the eye of someone who "in her place" would have done things differently. However, this suddenly easy life didn't smooth any corners or heal any rifts. She and her daughter continued to be on one side, and the *others* on the other side. She made two exceptions: one for Gabriela, to whom she owed everything; the other for her aunt, Júlia de Duarte. I don't include myself. My situation was different. We had long since stopped seeing each other, and only chance would bring us together again, on a street in the Chiado district of Lisbon. I therefore knew nothing about her married life. I'd met her when she was single and when I met her again she was a widow.

In the olden days, some women would shut themselves away in their houses for good when their husbands died. Some didn't even let the sun in, perhaps because they would find its cheerful face too shocking. Dora Rosário went to work, showed her few customers around the various pieces of stylish antique furniture and trinkets from a bygone age, then had lunch in a café or at a snack bar, and occasionally smoked a cigarette with her coffee, but, when she returned home at the end of the day, it was as if she had never left. Even after ten years of widowhood, she still wore black, and, given the long full skirts she wore and the sensible shoes, she looked more like an off-duty nun than what she actually was—a career widow. The post-prandial cigarette was almost as shocking to see as the smooth white arms of certain old ladies, whose faces and hands have been left weathered and lined by age. People did sometimes look at her and perhaps smile. Not that Dora Rosário cared, because the image of her husband had accompanied her since the morning, was there with her on the metro, and returned home at her side. It was an image that had lost much of its intensity. Time had, inevitably, eaten away at it, but so slowly that, for the most part, that natural erosion didn't really bother her much. The image would last as long as it lasted, and that was enough.

Gabriela had once spoken to Dora about her husband, but this was before Dora Rosário took the job in the store, in the very worst time, just a few months after his death. This was when Dora was only leaving the house to do the painful daily round of checking the newspaper ads or begging for work or money. They were sitting opposite each other, and Gabriela was sympathizing with her in a tactful way. "It's you I feel sorry for. He would never ask for a raise because he found it too humiliating. *Asking* for something, how terrible! No, he preferred to make do on very little, to scrape by. Now you're the one who has to go around asking, and not just of one person, but many, now you're the one who has to suffer that humiliation." Or something along those lines, as Gabriela herself told me later. Dora had immediately bridled, eyes glittering. Gabriela shrugged then and backed off: "All right, all right, forget I spoke. Forgive me if I offended you, I certainly didn't mean to…"

Dora Rosário, meanwhile, was thinking, and on her thin lips—sometimes so thin as to be barely visible—there was a slightly disdainful smile. These stupid people would never understand that she knew all this, that when he was still alive, when he was alive with no "still" hanging over him, she had thought exactly the same thing a thousand times over and kept silent a thousand times too. She had constantly been on the point of telling him. She never had, of course, because she lacked the courage. Had she said anything of the sort, it would have spoiled everything, and he would have looked at her, horrified, suddenly realizing that she—his wife— was, after all, a vulgar creature like all the others who had never understood him, or still worse that she had always secretly been against him. And that wasn't true. No, it wasn't. She *was* him, and always had been, even though in that single body formed of two bodies there might be a few rebellious molecules.

One day, after they were already married, Duarte had said to her: "I'm not the kind of man who wants to rise in the world at the expense of others, or indeed of myself. That smacks too much of wheeling and dealing, and I'm not and never will be a dealer in anything. Nor am I going to stand up in the marketplace listing my many qualities and putting a price on them. I just let myself drift, that's all I can do and all I want to do."

"Other men are willing to put a price on their talents."

"They live in the jungle and need a diet of fresh meat."

"So do you. You *are* fresh meat, but getting less fresh by the day. You don't even try to run away. You refuse to see that it *is* the jungle. For you, it's a paradise that you don't want to lose."

This is what she thought but did not say. She merely listened attentively to his brief didactic speeches and thought of the answers she longed to give him. Sometimes, though, it was as if Duarte could hear her thoughts.

"Oh, I can see the wild beasts," he would say. "I know them, can smell them. Don't go thinking that I can't tell a vulture from a pigeon. I simply ignore the vultures, that's all. I walk past at a distance. I refuse to look at them."

"But they exist. And while they may not devour us, they devour the food that should be ours."

"I refuse to join in," he went on. "Let them rot if they want to, *I* will remain intact. *We*," he added, correcting himself, "will remain intact."

Intact, thought Dora. *Good grief, intact.*

I, he had said. How often had he uttered that pronoun *I*. And even when he corrected himself and said *we*, he was still thinking *I*. An egotistical Christ, she used to think; a secular, unbelieving Christ who had only come into the world in order to save himself. But save himself from what, from what hell? She felt no bitterness, though, when she thought all this, only a slight bittersweetness, or a secret sense of contentment because she did love him. He was a good man, a pure man, untouched by the surrounding malice and greed. He remained uncontaminated. And Dora felt rather bad about being so critical of him—not entirely believing in his abstract idols and failing wholeheartedly to admire his saintly ways—and instead eyeing with a sly smile the invisible pedestal on which he had placed himself.

One day, when their daughter had just turned two, Dora said to her husband: "It's normal for women to go out to work these days, and I could get a job somewhere or other, it would certainly help. I saw in the newspaper that…"

He immediately interrupted her. What non-sense. What about the child? Was she going to hand her over to some stupid nanny? Besides, whatever she earned would only go to the nanny, who would then fritter it away. He paused, then looked at her hard. He gave her enough money, didn't he?

Dora nodded, not daring to say that she knew how little he ate for lunch and how poorly, and that he walked for miles rather than spend money on trams. She said nothing, not wanting to hurt his feelings, and she never did say any-thing, right up until the end, because there came a point when, if she had spoken out, he would have thought she had never been on his side, but had always been on the other side, among his critics.

One day, her mother-in-law said to her: "I don't know why you don't get a job. Duarte doesn't earn very much and he's unlikely ever to earn much more. Besides, every little bit helps." And Dora then found herself explaining that she couldn't just hand her daughter over to some

stupid nanny, demonstrating to her mother-in-
law, with examples and numbers, that all or almost all her earnings would simply be frittered
away by the nanny. Her mother-in-law smiled
faintly and said: "That's just what Duarte would
say"—end of conversation.

Her mother-in-law was about fifty but
looked older. She had a broad, beaky face, very
white and heavily powdered, with huge yellow
eyes and long eyelashes—almost indecently long
for a woman her age—very lined skin, and hair
that had once been blonde and that, in a heroic
battle against time, continued to be. She wore too
much makeup as well, which was often slightly
smudged because her eyesight wasn't what it had
been (worn-out machine, she would say, a little
rusty—just a little—urgently in need of replacement parts, but where to find them?). She always
wore heavy dangly earrings, which dragged
down her soft earlobes, and, on her right ring
finger, a glittering, multifaceted diamond.

Later, when she was already in her fifties, she
said to Dora with the impersonal air she sometimes adopted (as if to say: "I'm only saying this
for your own good, and if you don't agree then I
wash my hands of the matter"):

"I think you should do something to help Duarte."

"Do something? Me?" Dora asked in alarm. "What more *can* I do?"

"You need to advise him, to point out to him all the many things he's intent on ignoring."

"And which he's always ignored."

"Always? Possibly," said her mother-in-law with a worldly air. Then she went on: "Tell him, for example, that work is a normal part of life. By letting yourself be drawn in, by agreeing with him, you're actually acting against his best interests."

"No, I'm not," said Dora. "I'm acting against my interests and against Lisa's. And what's even worse: I know I am."

"But why?"

"Because I really love Duarte," she said wearily and almost on the brink of tears.

Her mother-in-law half closed her large eyes, and then she did look terribly old. Old and fixed as a death mask. "Perhaps you're right," she said. "It may be so, but I really don't think that's what he needs. I really don't."

Her mother-in-law was to blame, as was her father-in-law when he was alive, and even, to some degree, Aunt Júlia. They were all guilty. But her mother-in-law was first in line. She had been what you might call the main tower of the fortress, from the day her husband was left paralyzed, wheelchair-bound, and unconscious. Well, almost unconscious, with only brief glimmers of life during that long-drawn-out death, death having bungled the final blow like some old executioner ripe for retirement. Dora thought, however, that even before her husband's illness, her mother-in-law had been first in line, because she was the one with the money and was both physically and morally stronger. Just as some people are born with broad shoulders and others with narrow shoulders, some with a loud voice and others with weak ones. Her shoulders had always been broad, and her sharp, cool, almost shockingly youthful voice scaled the highest mountains with no apparent difficulty. And, of course, because she had money—don't forget the money—she had grown accustomed to being in charge and to being obeyed. Almost always obeyed. Her mother-in-law would have liked Duarte to be everything, but he turned out to be nothing. This was perhaps the sole activity, if you can call it that, to which he had gladly devoted his life—to being nothing. He had abandoned his engineering degree right at the start because he simply had no vocation for it. The people who knew him well, Gabriela for example, told me that it was simply not credible that Duarte could ever have become an engineer. Duarte and numbers, Duarte and concrete things, even abstractly concrete things…never. He has no vocation for engineering, the family would say. Duarte-who-has-no-vocation-for-engineering…but what *did* Duarte have a vocation for? Gazing at stars through a telescope or at microbes through a microscope might conceivably have been suitable occupations for Duarte. However, no one ever thought of that, not even him, and he ended up (only because someone found him a job) as a pen-pusher in some company that made soap, thus cutting short any hopes his mother might have had, for she had always said that her son would one day cause a stir. She had never provided any basis for such a prediction, that he was intelligent, for example, or any other more or less valid reason. That woman—who, as she herself said, had been born with a silver spoon in her mouth, and whom nothing, perhaps for that very reason, could ever frighten or surprise—had ended up with a son who would only be someone because he was her son. That business about the silver spoon was, of course, just one of her many rhetorical flourishes. Dora sometimes tried to penetrate that unknowable past, where she had never been, imagining conversations and constructing scenes, and where the father naturally also appeared on stage, although only as a secondary character. Secondary? No, not even that. A vast distance separated the tower from the other parts of the fortress. He was perhaps an echo, quietly repeating her proclamations. "You will be someone!" exclaimed that clear, full voice, which did in fact seem to descend from above, to fill large rooms, to linger for longer than was natural. "…someone!" repeated the echo. "Even if I have to…" – "…have to" added the modest, familiar, ever obliging echo.

Even if she had to… However, she had either failed or refused to take into account Duarte's vast reserves of passive resistance. He didn't argue with her, he merely looked at that mother who, for many years, had appeared to be indestructible, and, as he had once said to Dora, his only thought was that he must do the exact opposite, so as not to inherit that proprietorial gaze that shifted constantly between greed and satiety. He felt not one iota of frustration, though, unlike Aunt Júlia. For him, life was a transient state (transient, but with nothing at the end of it), of no use to anyone. Ambitions and struggles merely made him smile. Before his father fell ill, he would sometimes say to Duarte: "When I die, I will bequeath to you an honest, unsullied name." What was the point of his father's modest pride in having an "unsullied name," or his mother's pride in *her* son simply because he was her son? He rather pitied those pathetic, nonsensical feelings of pride. He, thought Dora, wasn't in the least bit proud. After all, a Christ, however egotistical, cannot be proud.

When Duarte died, and Dora realized that he was lost forever, it was as if the earth around her shook, and only the tiny scrap of earth beneath her feet remained still. Her world, already sparsely and rather poorly populated, was suddenly deserted. The arrival of Duarte in her life hadn't seen an expansion of her interests, but rather a complete replacement of them. His coming had automatically driven out everything that had, until then, filled her existence. She used to go to exhibitions, lectures, go dancing, visit friends at their houses (those friends she had either inherited or won in life's roulette game), and they would visit her too, in her small studio in the Príncipe Real quarter of Lisbon (her family lived in the provinces) where she would regale them with cakes and lemonade, and even an occasional glass of the delicious liqueur her

mother used to make. Duarte, though, had rendered all those things utterly uninteresting. She
began to view exhibitions as basically snobbish
(for the truth is she knew nothing about art), lectures as an act of self-flagellation that she found
easy enough to abandon, and her friends, whom
she still saw now and then, as boring and inau-
thentic.

On the day when the doctor told her Duarte
was dying (and that it would be best if he died
quickly so as to avoid any further unnecessary
suffering), before solitude spread all around her,
she felt stunned and wretched. She would hear
Duarte say, "Give me your hand," and think how
the voice with which he said those words would
die along with his body, and then she would re-
sist that idea and focus solely on that voice, as if to
render it immune to putrefaction, to lock it away
inside herself. Just as she did with his dull, hesi-
tant gaze, his gaunt face, and the hand—clammy
with sweat—that held her hand. She would say,
smiling: "The doctor thought you seemed a bit
better, love." Duarte, though, would look at her
vaguely, as if those words spoken with such con-
viction touched him only very lightly, or as if a
part of him were already in a place where there

could be no deceit, or as if the actual meaning of her words eluded him.

Dora Rosário loved him more than anything in the world. More than she loved her parents (who, by then, were dead), more than her seven-year-old daughter, more than herself. When he died, Dora found her life transformed into a desert. She found being alone painful; after all, she was only human, but at the same time, she wanted to be still more alone in order to suffer more, more completely, to spend more time thinking about Duarte, thinking more deeply, without other people's insignificant eyes sullying his image. She wanted her grief to remain uncontaminated. She woke from this grief, very briefly, to discover that she had only the monthly paycheck that Duarte's boss had sent to her house with "his deepest condolences." Nothing more. And thus began her calvary, her daily round: the newspaper ads, Senhor Black, Duarte's friends, acquaintances, work colleagues, and, of course, her in-laws.

"If you don't want to come, that's up to you, but at least drop off the little one. She can eat all she wants. Seven is a dangerous age, and she's not strong," her mother-in-law said.

Dora ended up leaving Lisa with her grandmother. She would go and see her every day
and didn't really miss her because her time was
entirely taken up with finding some solution to
her economic problems and with thinking about
Duarte. She would, of course, think about him
anyway, but she would also make a conscious
decision to do so. She would say to herself: "Now
I have a little time, I'll think about him." And she
would. Sitting in a chair or lying in bed in the
middle of the night, as motionless as a wax figure. She did this more or less religiously for ten
whole years.

At the time, she spent the mornings running here, there, and everywhere. Then, if it
was a nice day (even though it was winter), she
would go and fetch Lisa after lunch and take her
to Campo Grande. One day (she told me this
when she came to see me in order to justify herself and her daughter, "We are as we are, don't
you agree? It's just the way we're born") she was
walking along hand in hand with Lisa—she, a
rather shabby woman all in black alongside Lisa,
a skinny little girl with long straight hair, dressed
to the nines by her doting grandmother—the
two of them entered a clearing furnished with

several benches and where there were other children playing. The sky was blue, and the sun was at its warmest for the time of year. On one of the benches sat an old woman, enjoying the warmth. She wasn't one of those shriveled old women, but a plump, flaccid type. She was absorbed in her own thoughts, a vaguely vegetative smile on her colorless, shapeless lips. She was doing some lacework or crochet, something requiring a ball of thread and needles, but she was so distracted that the ball of thread had fallen onto the sandy ground. Lisa had stopped to stare, wrinkling her little nose. Then she had pointed her finger: "Look at her!" she said indignantly.

Dora Rosário had tugged hard at her hand, saying: "It's rude to point, you know."

"Why?"

"Because it is. Besides, that lady might see you and feel offended. Come on, it's getting late."

Lisa, however, refused to budge. She seemed fascinated. Her yellow eyes (or hazel, as people say now that she's a young woman) remained fixed on the bench, and in a firm and admonishing voice, she declared: "She's not a lady, she's an old woman."

Dora patiently explained to her that one shouldn't judge people by their appearance, and that one shouldn't say "old woman," but "elderly lady." Or, at most, "elderly person." Lisa, however, always had her own ideas, and her opinions were frank and forthright, even then, when she wasn't yet eight years old.

"She's a woman," she said, adding triumphantly, "an old woman! She's not a lady at all. Ladies dress like ladies. Ana is an old *lady*."

If Ana, Dora's mother-in-law, had heard this, she wouldn't have been at all pleased with that description. As far as she was concerned, only rags got old. This was her one concession to the deposit of rust that time left on all machines. Before she went into mourning, she had worn inappropriately garish colors. She had always cultivated a certain eccentricity and continued to do so even after her son's death. Black proved helpful though, and even lent her a certain dignity. Despite her sixty years, her permed, blonde hair, her paralyzed, semi-gaga husband incapable of stringing a sentence together, and her dead son, she remained very active and had lost none of her zest for life. She played canasta with three women friends, who were equally keen players, she drank a little more gin than was advisable for her heart, and she told anecdotes that made her friends laugh, because she really was very witty. The presence in the house of her granddaughter provided a new stimulus. She had studied Lisa closely and had discovered, to her great delight, that her granddaughter had not inherited *her father's unfortunate disposition, God rest his soul.* While she was not herself a believer, she was polite and well brought up (the silver spoon and all that) and was equally polite to God. She often said things like *God willing, God help me,* and *my God* and, now that her son had died, she frequently used and abused that expression *God rest his soul.* Anyway, it was true that Lisa had not inherited her father's unfortunate disposition. "Nor her mother's," Ana was quick to add, if Dora wasn't there. "I think she's going to turn out just like me," she would declare with a triumphant air. Then she would turn to Lisa: "What do you think? Would you like that?"

Lisa would gaze in some horror at her grandmother's painted mask of a face, nod affirmatively, and say diplomatically: "Yes, Ana," because even as a child, she knew what you should and shouldn't say in certain situations.

The granddaughter called her grandmother Ana. Her son had called her that too, but her daughter-in-law, since she had no mother, called her Senhora Dona Ana. And all because only rags grew old.

Then Dora got that job. Lisa came back to live with her, and thus life continued for ten years, with no major difficulties. Ten years during which Dora Rosário aged slightly, and during which her daughter became a young woman, growing ever more charming, ever prettier. She spoke English like an Englishwoman and spoke fairly good German too. She had less time for French. She was in eleventh grade and might well go on to college. Or would she instead become an airline stewardess? As for the image of Duarte, that grew less real over those ten years, but not alarmingly so. In order to survive, all it needed was the daily nourishment provided by Dora Rosário, obliging that image to live side by side with her, at home, in the street, in the shop.

The shop was called Matusalém, after Senhor Matos, the shop's owner and founder, but Lisa called it the Museum, and the name stuck. At home, Dora would say: "Today at the Museum…" – "This year at the Museum all I've sold…" – "We had a visitor to the Museum today…" There it was, the Museum.

It happened on a spring day like any other. Dora Rosário always closed the Museum at seven o'clock. Since, at that hour, there were never any customers, she had sent her assistant home and closed the door on yet another tedious day. She had spent the best part of the last ten years there, among tables large and small, some semicircular and propped against the wall, others like long-legged birds, half-asleep and slightly unsteady on their feet, others standing imperiously on sturdy legs with strong metal claws gripping the floor.

There were also sundry writing desks and a tall, delicate Etienne Avril escritoire, chests dating from various centuries, a solitary Regency lounge chair, its upholstery wearing thin, and many other pieces of furniture, all with very full curriculum vitae and all devoured by generations of energetic woodworms, but still very solid, gathered together like decaying aristocrats in a home for superior elderly folk. Glass domes covering beautiful clocks that had long since stopped, images from the eighteenth century, ornate boxes, exquisite, elegant ivory figurines, odd plates held together with metal brackets, a fine Persian rug, and, scattered here and there on the walls, frozen after many years in flight, were a profusion of Baroque angels, chubby and cheerful, modestly veiled or else fully clothed and even wearing boots, all of them with their bird wings spread. It was there in the Museum—because it really was more museum than shop, since it had more visitors than buyers—that Dora spent her days.

As a conscientious employee aware of her duties, she was always the last to leave. And that day was no exception. As usual, she said: "You can go now, Tomás" and he—like every other assistant she had ever had—didn't wait to be told again. He was, besides, ready to leave. When the only working clock in the shop (or the one that actually *was* still working) indicated seven o'clock, he had positioned himself close to the exit, waiting for Dora Rosário's immortal words. The only thing she did differently this time was that, instead of taking the subway, she hailed the first cab she saw and even told the driver she was in a hurry.

I don't know whether the image of Duarte accompanied her or not, she didn't mention it on the day she came to my place in order to talk. The calm waters of an apparently stagnant river can, at a certain point, form a torrent but then, later, continue serenely on their way. I don't think Dora Rosário ever recovered *her* serenity, but that's another story. As for the image of Duarte, it's possible that she had, for the first time, left it behind on one of the chairs in the Museum. Her daughter had invited a group of friends over, who would probably still be there. Later that evening, her grandmother and Aunt Júlia would be coming to supper. It was a special day for Dora Rosário: it was Lisa's seventeenth birthday and this was her first proper party. At the same time, it was the official debut, if I can put it like that, of the velvet-upholstered sofa and armchairs that Lisa had been nagging her to buy for ages "because I couldn't possibly invite anyone over to sit on those ugly old things, it would be too embarrassing."

Despite spending her days among beautiful furnishings, or perhaps for that very reason, Dora Rosário took little interest in what her own apartment looked like. Her husband had never given much importance to appearances and, naturally, if unwittingly, she had followed in his footsteps in that respect too. She was the kind of female who goes back to her cave or her den to rest among her children. But rest from what, when she was never really tired? But that's of no interest here. As long as she had a comfortable bed to sleep in and a heater in winter—because she did feel the cold—she didn't care about anything else. Lisa, on the other hand, had been to her girlfriends' homes, taken an interest in the decaying old aristocrats stored in the Museum, and was ashamed of their apartment. It had been necessary, therefore, to grant her wish.

As soon as Dora turned the key in the lock and went in, she heard the noise. Someone had brought a record player, and they were all dancing enthusiastically to a tune, if you could call it that, which was simultaneously raucous and syncopated and which she thought horrible. She went straight to the living room, and Lisa, who was always very affectionate (or so Dora said), immediately left her dancing partner and rushed over to embrace her. "Mom!" she cried. All her friends came and shook her hand while Lisa told her their names, and the young man on the record continued his bawling at regular intervals. There were five boys and four girls, and Dora saw at once that Lisa was by far the prettiest, although one of them, Madalena, was certainly very charming. Lisa, though, was tall and slim, had a neat little face with plump cheeks, long, very straight fair hair, and those large yellow, or rather, golden eyes, like sequins glittering in the light, her grandmother's eyes in a young girl's face.

Dora Rosário said: "Go on, don't worry about me," and made as if to leave. One of the boys, however, a snubnosed youth, asked her very sweetly to stay a while. Why didn't she sit down? She hesitated. She had to go and help the maid prepare supper (a special supper on that special day, with turkey, because both Lisa and Ana loved turkey), but the truth is she was tempted. They seemed so healthily happy! The boy, whose name was Jaime, brought her a glass of orange juice, and said with an almost apologetic smile, that it was all they had, since the mistress of the house (and he pointed at Lisa) had forgotten the whisky. Then he sat down beside her, still talking about Lisa.

Someone put on another record, and a couple started dancing—a tall redhaired girl with a statuesque body and a lot of freckles who went to the same dance school as Lisa, and a cheerful, skinny boy wearing glasses and with a slightly Asian look about him. It was a new dance (the twist or the surf perhaps, Dora didn't know), that involved the whole body. The dance didn't come from the outside in (and never really got "inside" anyway, limiting itself to mechanical gestures), as they used to when she was a girl; when a boy would ask: "Do you want to dance?" and the girl would answer, "Yes," and then the couple would move off, taking small, unthinking, conventional steps, chatting as they did so. This was entirely different. The dancers would be talking and laughing, and then, when the record started and while they were still talking and laughing, something inside them, in their blood let's say, would begin to take shape, like antibodies engendered by the music, which then proliferated (but much faster than was normal, until they, in turn, became a sickness), and then the couple would move and squirm, talking all the while, still unaware, or apparently unaware. But when they finally realized what they were doing, when their gestures took on a rhythm too powerful to be ignored, then they forgot everything and surrendered completely. It was like an African dance, long, repetitive, almost ritualistic, which held them in a trance until the final chord broke the spell.

When this happened and the chubby smiling girl, who had been placed in charge of the record player because she had sprained her ankle a few days earlier, put on something quieter, Jaime asked Dora Rosário if she would like to dance, and everyone giggled in a friendly fashion. Lisa exclaimed: "My mother dance? You must be mad! You obviously don't know her!" And laughing a little herself, Dora said that it had been such a long time since she'd danced that she didn't even know which hand to give to her partner.

The Asian-looking boy said in a high voice: "Hands? You don't need hands now! Or only by chance and very occasionally!" And everyone happily laughed even more.

Then Dora got up and explained that she had a lot to do, a family supper to prepare, and shook each of their hands and said what a pleasure it had been to meet Lisa's friends. Then she left, slowly closing the door. Someone said very quietly: "She's really nice, your mom…but it's odd, she doesn't seem like your mom." – "And she's not that old," added another voice, that of Madalena. "But there's something about her… How old is she?" Lisa immediately said: "I'm not sure. Thirty-five, thirty-eight maybe. Yes, I think she's thirty-eight, but my mother is both ageless and hopeless." Madalena said very slowly: "Yes, but she seems…I don't know, there's a kind of antique air about her. My mother's forty— you've all met her—and she could pass for my sister." The Asian-looking boy cried in a shrill voice that mothers were mothers, period. Everyone applauded, but above the applause, Dora Rosário heard Lisa say something about antiqueness being an occupational hazard. Immediately afterward or even simultaneously, though, the chubby girl at the record player announced: "The Beatles!" who then burst into song.

Dora Rosário walked slowly down the corridor, heading for the dining room, where she began, mechanically, to set the table. While doing this, she remembered Lisa's diary, which she had happened upon and opened months before. In that diary, among other youthful, almost rudimentary thoughts on her friends and on love (about which she clearly had her doubts), Lisa had written something that Dora suddenly remembered now and which came more or less to this: "When I was little, my mother used to invent stories for me that never left me feeling comforted or satisfied, because they were always the opposite of what they should have been, and most ended badly. In those stories, the witches were always pretty and clever, while the poor girls were just that, poor and ugly, inelegant and hopeless. They were even sometimes, if not often, downright bad, and that really complicated matters. What does it mean to have a happy ending or a sad one? And yet my mother *was* happy at the time. Or had Dad already died by then? I can't quite remember. Besides, she's not inelegant and, in her day, she wouldn't have been ugly either, although she does have very hopeless eyes. Hopeless eyes and a woman's body. Or am I being unfair?"

Dora had been astonished when she'd read those words. Had Lisa been there at the time, she would have slapped her. Later, once she calmed down, she realized that this would have been an overreaction. It was simply that, because she spent all of her days in a museum waiting for people who never came, she didn't really know her daughter. She didn't have time. Lisa, though, had a keen, observant mind, and there was nothing wrong with that, was there? So what if she observed her, her mother, with a critical eye? Poor scholars had to use whatever material was on hand. And if Lisa was using her without her knowledge, then so be it. Why shouldn't she be her daughter's guinea pig? And not wanting to reveal to her daughter that she had read her diary, she preferred to say nothing. And she gradually forgot about it. Indeed, she had forgotten it completely until Lisa said: "My mother is both ageless and hopeless." There had been a hint of humor in her voice, but that was fairly typical of Lisa. There was no suggestion of complaint in those words, it was merely a slightly ironic comment. She would have used exactly the same tone if she'd said: "What can my poor mother possibly expect from life, given her age and the way she dresses? Whereas we…"

As soon as she had finished setting the table, Dora went into the kitchen to make a fruit salad. Then she washed her hands and gave her hair a quick brush. She had neat, regular features, but had never done anything to help nature. Never. She seemed, rather, to be unconsciously intent on hampering it. You could describe her face as lackluster: matte skin, pale lips, dull, straight brown hair tied back at the nape of her neck. Only her eyes made that constant to-and-fro between life and death. Lisa was right that her body had perhaps always been her best feature, but she took so little trouble over how she dressed that even her body went unnoticed.

At half past eight, Ana and Aunt Júlia arrived, each bearing a present: the former brought a woolen sweater; the latter chocolates and two pairs of stockings. Ana was resplendent in her latest outfit, black lace, cultured pearl necklace, with her ever-thinner, ever-blonder hair. Her skin resembled old parchment and she certainly had not stinted on the makeup. By then, Lisa's friends had left, leaving her various gifts, books and a few records (Dora had promised to buy her a record player once she passed her exams), and Lisa herself was wandering around, cheerfully humming a song in English, virtually ignoring her grandmother and her aunt.

"Go and talk to them, go on!" Dora said when they passed each other in the corridor. "I just need to check that the food's ready."

Lisa snorted: "Have you seen Ana? She looks like a Toulouse-Lautrec painting, you know, that one you had a reproduction of at the Museum? Hasn't anyone ever told her that at her age... well, that, with all that makeup on, she looks like the madam of a brothel?"

Dora Rosário couldn't quite imagine what the madam of a brothel would look like, because she had always lived—both pre- and post-Duarte, and even during-Duarte—in a bacteriologically pure atmosphere, far from all such unsavory things, even as vague generalizations. Lisa, though, despite having turned seventeen just half an hour ago, knew precisely what she was talking about, of that Dora had no doubt. Ever since she was a child, she had possessed what you might call a sixth sense about those things and spoke confidently about them prior to having any actual knowledge of them. Dora said rather too quickly and glibly: "Don't talk about your grandmother like that." Lisa laughed her frank,

still childish laugh, and corrected her: "You
mean Ana." – "All right, Ana, if you like." Lisa
shrugged and said: "It's not me, it's her. She's the
one who wants to be called Ana. Besides, why
shouldn't I say Ana resembles an ancient cock-
atoo?" And with that she went into the living
room where the two women were waiting for
her with their presents, their usual wet kisses and
congratulatory hugs accompanied by the inevitable wishes for "many happy returns."

Ana did full justice to the supper and praised
the turkey, immediately asking Dora to give her
a bit of breast to take back to "poor José." Afterward they drank champagne. Aunt Júlia got
over-excited and drank three glasses, and then just
as she was about to down a fourth, she had one
of her attacks, yet another one. She was quite a
lot younger than her sister, but she didn't dye her
hair, which was now completely white. She was
a small, serene, pleasant woman, slightly stooped,
and never a great talker. A hieroglyph that was
more like a meaningless doodle. She'd had a
husband, she'd had children, but all had long since
died, and she spent her days embroidering things
for Lisa's trousseau or reading romantic novels.
She gladly allowed herself to be organized by

Ana and was very solicitous to "poor José," never forgetting to give him his medicines on time and push his wheelchair closer to the window when it was sunny. However, Aunt Júlia was subject to frighteningly violent fits and therein lay her mystery. Afterward, under the influence of the drug she was given, and which she always, very sensibly, kept in her handbag, she would start rambling, talking to some man, with her supplying both sides of the conversation. He was someone they had all, apart from Aunt Júlia, tried to forget (they weren't even allowed to mention his name), a lover by whom she'd had a son (who, fortunately, had died very young). Dora Rosário found the attacks suffered by this otherwise very serene woman almost heartbreaking. Aunt Júlia's belly would gradually start to rise and fall faster, like water beginning to boil, and they would all grab hold of her (as they did that evening) by the wrists and feet, protecting her head; then her back would suddenly go rigid, horizontal, as if she were floating three feet above the floor, free from the force of gravity, and she would then writhe with alarming intensity, almost unfeasible in such an apparently frail creature. Then, little by little, she would relax, and remain absent and still, lips closed, until, minutes later, it would happen again. Once they managed to get her to take her medicine, she would sleep for hours on end, and in her sleep, they would talk, her and him, the man-with-no-name, arguing or murmuring sweet nothings. At a certain point, though, she would reach out and scratch anyone who happened to be near, would tear at the sheets, bite. And she would scream at him to go away, saying she never wanted to see him again. "Go away, you wretch!" Every one of Ana's long succession of maids had the same opinion: Senhora Dona Júlia was clearly possessed by the Devil, and they really ought to call a priest. This was a view shared by Dora's maid too, as she stood there exhausted, her apron all torn, when Aunt Júlia had finally calmed down.

Ana treated her sister with the mechanical gestures of a specialist nurse, feeling neither shock nor sorrow, as if Aunt Júlia had a problem with her kidneys or her liver. All she asked was that the others hold on tight, so that the poor woman did not hurt herself. Dora, however, never got used to it, despite having witnessed several such attacks. This was Lisa's first experience of the spectacle, however, and she watched wide-eyed so as not to miss a thing.

"Senhora Dona Júlia must be possessed by the Devil," said Dora's maid breathlessly.

"Oh, be quiet and don't talk such nonsense!" retorted Ana. "Go and wash up and make yourself a strong cup of coffee. That's what you need. And leave me to take care of the Devil."

Ana did not believe in God or the Devil, she was a natural rationalist, albeit entirely untutored, but she knew, instinctively, that her sister had piled up an infinite storehouse of memories and that everything that came after "that affair"—husband, children, their respective lives and death—had found her slightly distracted, absorbed in her own thoughts.

Dora felt great sympathy for Aunt Júlia. And when, that night, before going to her room, Lisa asked, "Was that an attack of hysteria?" And then, "…but why didn't she…I mean why didn't she just get married?" Dora responded almost angrily, telling her to go to bed and stop asking stupid questions. She had always, in a way, felt drawn to that lover who could not be named and to the child who died when only two years old (to the family they were always *that man* and *the child*). When Duarte, before they were married, told her the story, he had concluded by saying more or less: "...then *that man* left her before *the child* was even born. *The child* died when he was only two from scarlet fever. It was lucky for her really."

Lucky. Aunt Júlia died one evening following another of those attacks, some time after Dora's visit to me. She died talking to the man-with-no-name, speaking to him in anguished terms of the child about to be born and of her deep shame. She had turned fifty the day before.

Dora spent the night of Lisa's birthday in the dim light of a lamp, sitting in one of the velvet-upholstered armchairs with her mother-in-law next to her on the sofa, covered by a quilt, while her own bed was occupied by Aunt Júlia, fast asleep and occasionally talking to the man-with-no-name. The maid had gone to her room, exhausted, and Lisa had retreated indignantly to hers.

Dora was staring, as if fascinated, at her mother-in-law's head, visible above the pink quilt, complete with makeup, disheveled blonde hair, and pendant earrings. It was as if someone had placed a papier-mâché mask on a pile of bedding. Her mother-in-law, meanwhile, was sleeping soundly, the quilt rising and falling gently in time with her regular breathing. However, at one point, without opening her eyes, she said:

"Dora…" – "What?" asked Dora, startled, because she had assumed she was asleep. Ana smiled, her eyes still closed: "People my age don't need much sleep, we just doze, that's all." And Dora Rosário was surprised because this was the first time Ana had ever referred to her age, especially right at the beginning of a conversation, with no prompting. "Dora…" she said again. "For ten years now, I've been meaning to talk to you about something important, but I've kept putting it off. And we've so rarely been alone together during those ten years. There's always someone: Júlia, Lisa, poor José, and though he may not understand much of what he hears, he's always needing something or other. Tonight, though, we're completely alone. It's now or never."

Then she fell silent, and after some time had passed, Dora assumed her mother-in-law must have changed her mind or forgotten what it was she had wanted to say, or she had perhaps fallen asleep again. This was not the case. She was simply choosing her words carefully. Cautiously. She clearly did not find this easy, because, after another long, expectant pause, she merely asked:

"Do you know what a fixation abscess is?"

"I don't know much about medicine," said

Dora, "but I think it's an abscess created artifi-
cially to draw in all the bacteria."

"Yes, I think that's it. Well, you need such an
abscess, and I'm the cruel doctor who's going to
create it and make you suffer."

"I don't understand."

Ana finally opened her eyes and raised herself up a little on one elbow. She still didn't look
at Dora, though. She seemed absorbed in herself,
her eyes turned inward. Then she spoke. Slowly,
like someone repeating a definition learned by
heart: "Shortly before he fell ill," she said, "Duarte
was thinking of leaving you and going to live
with another woman."

"That can't be true!" cried Dora, so loudly
that Aunt Júlia stirred in her bed and began
talking again, her eyes no doubt glinting darkly,
ready to hurl herself on the enemy, biting him
and tearing off lumps of flesh.

"It can," said Ana calmly. "It can. He spoke
to me about it and even told me who the woman
was. A work colleague of his, I think, although
I can't remember her name anymore. He'd made
up his mind. For once in his life, he was going to
take the initiative, a real novelty. I'm sorry to say
this, but I didn't try to dissuade him. I thought

perhaps that other woman might make something of him. But then he fell ill, and never left
his bed. She came to see me one day to ask how
he was, but never came back. She was a small,
nervous woman, like a very intelligent mouse."

"So he didn't love me…" murmured Dora.

Ana shrugged. "Perhaps he loved you too,
but slightly less, you never know with men. The
poor things were made to have a harem in which
all the women would get along as happily as God
does with the angels, but the Holy Church put
a stop to that. What are men supposed to do?
Accumulate various women or leave one woman
for another, although that's less common nowadays…anyway, nothing could be more normal.
Why, even poor José…"

Ana was talking, but Dora wasn't listen-
ing. For the first time in her life, she felt utterly
alone. Not alone, but adrift in a boat, with no
sails, no oars, no wind, marooned on a motionless sea. This was a nightmare, from which she
would surely soon wake up, and find everything
in its proper place: the image of Duarte, her role
as inconsolable widow, those moments when
she would summon up his presence. Suddenly,
though, there was nothing: only a woman more

deceived than any other, deceived beyond death itself for ten whole years.

She still managed to respond angrily: "You're just inventing things to make me suffer! Why? What harm did I ever do to you?" And her eyes glittered aggressively.

Ana, however, lay down again, closed her bluish eyelids, and gave a deep, deep sigh, like someone who has had a great weight lifted off her.

"Say what you like. It's only to be expected really, inevitable. The mother-in-law who loathes the first wife who stole her son from her and prefers his mistress to his legitimate wife. It's classic. But listen, I've never loathed anyone. Do you think I would invent something like this?"

No, she wouldn't, and Dora knew that. She got a grip on herself and said softly: "I'm sorry." Then she thought for a while and added: "I don't think I'm going to be able to create a different situation now. I was used to the old one, it was comfortable. At the moment, I don't know where I am or who I am. I must be crumbling into pieces, there must be bits of me all over the place."

"Sweep them up when you're feeling brave enough and put them together again."

"Yes, that's what I have to do, isn't it?" Dora said, not even thinking about what she was saying. And then immediately afterward, her voice rose dangerously in volume: When would she, too, fall and shatter? It was as if she had lost control of herself and of her voice. Or perhaps it was as if she were screaming for help from inside a coffin that had just that minute been nailed shut: "Why didn't you either keep quiet about it or tell me sooner? You could always have come to see me at the shop!" Then she saw that this would have been impossible. "No, not in the shop, but here, on a Sunday, when Lisa was at the cinema, or you could have asked me over to your house, to your bedroom. Your bedroom has a lock, doesn't it?"

"Yes, but the walls are very thin."

Ah, she should have thought of that. This would have to be yet another secret between them. Like *that man* and *the child*. Ana might still know the name of the woman in question, but Dora would never get it out of her (and what would be the point?). She was now *that woman* and would be ever more. Despite Ana not having tried to dissuade Duarte and despite thinking she resembled a very intelligent mouse, despite all of that.

Dora heard her say: "At least my conscience can rest easy. It has nothing to do with me now." She gave another very deep sigh, like someone about to plunge into a long silence. But then she did go on to say: "I think I'm going to sleep for a bit. Why don't you do the same? Go and lie down with Lisa, that would be best." And with some difficulty, because she was fat and the sofa narrow, she turned onto her other side.

My mother is both ageless and hopeless. Have you seen Ana? Has no one ever told her she looks like the madam of a brothel? Duarte was planning to leave you and go and live with another woman. Why didn't Aunt Júlia just get married? She's both ageless and hopeless. Has no one ever told Ana? Duarte wanted to go and live with another woman. He died with you at his side, but he wanted to live with another woman. With *that woman*, a work colleague, I can't remember her name now, she resembled a very intelligent mouse. My mother is both ageless and hopeless. The Museum... An occupational hazard... Do you know what a fixation abscess is? Duarte was planning... Duarte wanted... Duarte was intending to... I'm sorry to say this, but I didn't try to dissuade him. For once in his life, he was going to take the initiative, a real novelty.

Later, when she told me about all this, she described in detail that vast, unreal night, with the ancient, painted effigy of her mother-in-law emerging from the pink quilt; Aunt Júlia in the bedroom, speaking of love to *that man* and responding for him in her sleep; and her, sitting in the velvet-upholstered armchair, suddenly alone, so alone that not even the existence of Lisa could console her. Then Ana had gone back to sleep, dozed off, and her aunt had fallen silent. Only she remained awake and wretched, sadder even than on the day Duarte died. Much sadder. She wanted to sleep, to escape herself, to escape the new life she would now be obliged to live, but the paths into sleep were more difficult, more complicated than ever. Cul-de-sacs, long rivers with no tributaries and no sea, no sources either, rocky mountains that she would have to scale in order to see over to the other side, to another landscape. She fell asleep, woke, slept again, and woke again. Before her lay her mother-in-law's face, almost deathly pale now, her skin having finally absorbed all the makeup—it was like the face of a corpse. And Dora Rosário wished Ana had died yesterday, or the day before yesterday, or a few hours

ago, before she'd had the chance to speak, before uttering those words which were, after all,
so unnecessary.

Two days later, I happened to drop by the Museum, something I did from time to time, whenever I was in the area with not much to do. She was always sitting at the back of the shop, a slightly more spacious area that formed a small room relatively separate from the more exposed body of the store that her assistant guarded with his mere presence. He spent most of the time leaning in the doorway, watching passersby. Weather permitting of course. On that particular spring day, there he was at his post.

I found Dora busily knitting, perhaps a sweater for her daughter. She was surrounded by all the more precious items, not because their presence gave her any pleasure, but because they were safer there. Opposite her, on a clawfoot pedestal table, the one-clock-that-worked—a beautiful French lyre clock in cobalt blue porcelain, its face encircled by imitation diamonds and ormolu decorations—was serenely marking the time, Dora Rosário's time, the clock's time, and all our time. On that day, however, Dora Rosário's time appeared to have stopped, and she looked at me as she did on her bad days, all emotion soaked up as if by blotting paper. I had never seen her eyes so dry and dim and dull as they were then. It was as if the light we all automatically turn on in order to see had suddenly blown out, and the outside world was no longer visible to her.

We talked about one thing and another, she mentioned that her daughter had turned seventeen two days before and showed me the photograph she kept in her handbag. I expressed the usual degree of amazement that one does on such occasions, but I genuinely did find her daughter very pretty. I said as much, and Dora responded with a vague "Yes, she is, isn't she?" with the air of someone whose thoughts are miles away. It was probably because there was absolutely nothing else to talk about that I spoke to her of my problem, feeling sure that she wouldn't pay much attention. I had spoken about it to her before, but never for as long as I did that afternoon when she wasn't really listening.

My problem always bore the same name, Ernesto—an old problem with nothing new about it. Dora was fairly familiar with the problem, although not with Ernesto, who, at the time, she had met only fleetingly on a couple of occasions, and from the little she said, I gathered that she didn't like him much. "He's a bit smug, isn't he?" she said immediately after one of those brief encounters. He was. And, I suppose, still is. And this was apparent in every aspect of his life, even in the overcoats he wore, the kind of coats that seem not so much tailored as sculpted, as I told him more than once. A man who wore such overcoats must feel himself to be like a statue, glory set in stone. As for Dora, Ernesto once referred to her (the only time he did until the day after the visit I'm describing) as "your Salvation Army friend."

I'm not going to reproduce here what I told Dora about my problem, and whenever I mention Ernesto, it will be purely in relation to her and her daughter. I'm not part of this story—if you can call it that—I'm a mere bit-part player of the kind that has not even a generic name, and never will have, not even in any subsequent stories, because we simply lack all dramatic vocation. At one point (and this *is* relevant), I mentioned

what was, for me, the ridiculous fact of him being in the process of furnishing his house up in
the hills around Sintra. "He knows perfectly well
that I don't want to go and live there, so… Anyway, he's looking for a rug now…do you have
any?" Dora, alas, did have rugs. And she showed
them to me in mechanical fashion. One of them
was a real beauty, exactly the kind of Persian rug
Ernesto was looking for. Slightly worn, it's true,
but that was almost a plus. Brand-new things
seem a touch nouveau-riche when the people
buying them are no longer particularly young.
In a rush of magnanimity, I decided to help
him furnish that house in which I had no desire
to live. After all, I might spend the occasional
weekend there.

"I'll ask him to pop in one of these days. How
much are you asking for it?"

Dora told me, and it was fairly pricey. Not
that this would be a problem for Ernesto, which
is why I said I'd give him the address. The assistant chipped in then to remind Dora that another customer had expressed interest, a German
lady, who had said she would come back with
her husband. Dora Rosário said: "Yes, you're
right. I'd forgotten about her." And she clapped

her hand to her forehead as if she suddenly felt a terrible pain. "If you think Dr. Laje really would be interested, then tell him to come tomorrow at the latest. If the German woman turns up, we'll make some excuse."

Ernesto did not turn up the following day, because the following day he had to go to Porto to defend a client. He came straight back, but it seems he was very busy, so much so that I barely saw him, and I'm only telling you this as a way of saying that he didn't manage to visit the Museum until some eight or ten days later, but the rug was still there, hanging on the wall. The German woman had apparently not returned.

That night, we went to supper at the Choupana, and I asked him: "Did you speak to Dora?" – "Dora who?" he said with the air of a man who isn't really there but somewhere else, doing something else, an air that had become all too familiar to me in recent weeks. "Dora Rosário," I said. And he repeated the name, like someone suddenly falling back to earth: "Oh, Dora Rosário, yes, I did speak to her. Tell me, has something happened to her?" Since I had no idea at the time what had happened, I told him that I didn't know, but that I, too, had found her strange. Although not that strange. "I mean, what happened to the Salvation Army look and all that?" he asked. "Oh, that," I said. Then some other more important matter came up and we didn't talk about her again. In fact, I didn't even ask him if he'd bought the rug. I felt I'd done enough. It was best not to overdo the magnanimity or it might look suspicious. Besides, a certain freedom of movement without interference on either side had become the norm in the life we'd chosen, or, rather, that he had chosen and to which I'd agreed. But let's not go there, because, as I said, I'm not part of this story.

Days later, I happened to be back in that part of town, so I dropped in at the Museum again. I was almost speechless with surprise. But there I am talking about myself and my trivial sensations again, which isn't at all my intention. I prefer to imagine events in accordance with what I know about Dora Rosário and Ernesto, and also in accordance with what Dora told me that day about herself and Lisa. Too bad if my imagination and my faulty memory distort reality. It might well have happened this way. Nothing could be more natural.

Precisely two days after Lisa's birthday and Dora's late-night conversation with her mother-in-law—that is, the same day I went to see her at the Museum—Dora Rosário left the shop early for the first time in ten years. This, however, had nothing whatsoever to do with my visit, as she herself insisted the day she came to see me. She had planned it all the previous day. As I was saying, she left the shop early, having first instructed her assistant, Tomás, to lock the door and drop the key off at her apartment.

That afternoon, she did various things. She bought a white blouse and a black suit, light-colored stockings and high heels. Then she went to a hairdresser's, which she had happened to find in the phone book and where she'd made an appointment, and she bought a few things she hadn't used since her husband died: lipstick, perfume, eyeliner. In the days that followed, she also bought some fabric and ordered a jacket and a few dresses to be made. Nothing very luxurious, but all very attractive. I would never have imagined Dora had such good taste. Indeed, she had always seemed determined to prove the opposite.

The result wasn't really so very amazing. More surprising was the fact that she'd done it at all. Dora Rosário, *the Salvation Army look and all that*, transforming into someone who looked just like the rest of us was truly unexpected. And yet...yes, when I think about it—and doing my best to be absolutely impartial—I have to admit that while she wasn't pretty exactly, she was rather attractive, and certainly looked a lot younger. It was as if she had suddenly regained those wasted ten years and was certainly making up for lost time.

The day of her transformation was also, she told me later, *the day of the conversation about youth*. Dora Rosário always categorized days according to their most important events. There had been *the day of the late-night conversation with her mother-in-law*, *the day of the conversation about youth*, and there would be *the day of the trip to*

Sintra, the day of the lunch in Cascais, and many others that grew in importance, becoming more important even than *the day of her wedding*.

That day, though, the day of her transformation (because the conversation had not yet taken place that would have even more importance in defining that day for Dora), she got home later than usual and was feeling slightly embarrassed, only to be welcomed by Lisa—well, let's imagine she was—with a wolf-whistle and genuine excitement.

"Wow! What happened to you?" She walked around her, wanting to view her from every angle. "You look great, fabulous!" she said. "I mean, to people your own age you would. And even to me…"

"Oh, so I'm still an old lady, am I?" Dora had said this without a smile, even with a hint of rancor.

"No, no, you look much younger, much much younger. And I'm really pleased. I've always had a bit of a complex, you know. Madalena's mother is still so pretty, so is Beca's, and Jaime's too…"

"Who's Jaime?" asked Dora simply for the sake of asking.

"The guy who sat next to you at the party. Have you forgotten already?"

So much had happened since Lisa's party, two days earlier, so many deaths. Then she remembered.

"Oh, I know the one. Is he a little in love with you?"

The question just came out like that, almost without her thinking, at least, it may have. The previous day she might not have been able to ask that question with such nonchalance, and Lisa might not have been so quick to answer:

"Yes, I think he is. He's never said anything, but I think he is."

"And what about you?" Dora said this with some trepidation, because the sudden idea of her daughter liking a man seemed almost monstrous. "What about you?" she asked again.

Lisa reassured her. She laughed and shrugged. "Don't worry. I like the fact that he's a little in love with me, but that's all. I still feel too young for unnecessary complications like that. I want to have fun." She remained thoughtful for a moment, then declared: "You know, Mom, I think that young people nowadays know something you never did. We know we have to enjoy life while we can. You…"

Dora said: "What do you know about *us*?"

"I can guess. We young people know that youth doesn't last very long, and you have to make the most of it because, by the time you're thirty, it's all over. Make the best of it, I mean. Perhaps with an eye to the future, because the future's important."

"You'll feel different when you reach thirty," said Dora, ignoring those last words. "You put off 'the end' until you're forty, then until you're fifty. That way, you'll never feel old."

"Is that what you think?"

"Me? Well…"

"What about *your* youth, though, where did that go?" Lisa asked, interrupting her. "It's been lost somehow. So…you, for example…you've been rejuvenated, which I think is great, but what have you gotten out of life? Until now, I mean…"

This was a difficult question to answer just then. Dora Rosário managed to control her feelings, though, and gave the answer she would have given before *the late-night conversation with her mother-in-law*: "I was happy with your dad."

Lisa was politely skeptical: "Yes, maybe. But do you think eight or ten years of happiness, if you want to call it that, is enough for a person's life? Then what happened? Nothing but hardship. You need to make the most of your *entire* life, that's what we young people think. I only want to fall in love with someone I want to fall in love with, someone who can guarantee me security, do you understand?"

Dora said: "No boy your own age can possibly do that, or only in very exceptional circumstances." And Lisa's response was rather dreamy, slightly sibylline: "Exactly."

Their rare, serious, mother-daughter conversations, like that one, always left a slightly bitter taste in her mouth. Her daughter seemed to know about life before she had even lived it, she seemed immune to fear before she had even encountered any reason to be fearful. She took everything in her stride, as if she had already considered everything from every angle and formed her own opinion. But then that's how she was in every situation. At school, she always got on the honor roll, and her teachers heaped praise on her. Yet Lisa, though conscientious, was not what you would call a keen student. Lately, whenever anyone asked her what she wanted to study in college, she would hesitate—she didn't really know. She still had time, lots of time. She might, for example, be tempted to become a stewardess… She'd have to see. It had to be a career that didn't involve doing the same thing every day, or even against the same backdrop.

The following Sunday, when, as usual, they went to supper at Ana's place, Ana eyed her daughter-in-law curiously and with a faint but eloquent smile. She said nothing though. Aunt Júlia, on the other hand, was full of enthusiastic cries and exclamations. Dora Rosário spent the whole evening waiting for her mother-in-law to say something, but whenever she looked at her, she found Ana looking back at her. Ana was normally in the habit of throwing out small, discreet hooks, so mingled with algae and slime that sometimes the fish didn't even spot it was a hook and would take the tasty or necessary bait. At other times, though, the fish could see the bait approaching, inch by inch—sometimes hiding behind the rocks before suddenly heaving into view—and the fish would simply ignore it. On that day, there was no bait, only searching, meaningful looks. Was she pleased with the result or shocked by how quickly her daughter-in-law had embraced her unspoken instructions? It was hard to know.

Dora and Lisa walked home, because they both enjoyed walking at night, especially in the spring, and Lisa broke the silence to ask:

"Is Ana part of your eight or ten years of happiness? I mean, is she a memory of Dad that you visit *religiously* on a weekly basis, the way you've hung on to his science fiction books, his pipe, and his stamps?"

"Why do you ask?"

Lisa laughed and squeezed her arm, as if she were talking to a child: "No reason, Mom, just so I can understand. Understand better. I like Ana because she's my grandmother, I've known her since I was little, and she gives me things, that's normal, but what's your connection to her?"

"It's hard to explain," said Dora Rosário. "But there are some things. You for one. Well, mainly you really."

"And does habit play a part?"

"Oh, yes, definitely."

"So basically, you have nothing in common. I mean, nothing more than that."

"Don't be so silly, Lisa. No one has anything in common with anyone, apart from blood ties, like you and me, for example, and even then…" She laughed and patted her gently on the back.

"What about Dad?" Lisa asked, smiling.

"Oh, yes, your dad, of course," Dora Rosário said rather limply. "Of course."

"That's why you didn't just dump Ana, or, rather, why you didn't allow her to dump you."

"Ana has never meddled in my life, Lisa."

Lisa laughed: "No, of course not, you just have to look at her eyes. Curious, disapproving, critical, or else suspicious. Today, they were suspicious, did you notice? You could have chosen to be free, but instead you stayed clinging to a remnant of Dad, to his mother."

Dora Rosário didn't even hear those last few words. She was still thinking about what she herself had said: "Ana has never meddled in my life." Oh, yes, she had, Dora thought. *On the day of the late-night conversation*, she had completely turned the tables on her and, in just a few words, had erased her image of Duarte, leaving her entirely alone. She had lost her own self-image too (voluntarily, or so she had thought, fool that she was), the image of herself she had grown accustomed to, and which had suited her because it had made her life easier. Oh, Ana had meddled all right! Thinking that she might have offended her mother, Lisa was looking at Dora with a rather concerned expression. Then she put her arms around her, right there in the deserted street: "I'm sorry, Mom. Keep your memories, keep Ana as well as the pipe. You know what I'm like. I just come out with these things. I think I'm rather like Ana in that way. Although whereas she just looks, I put my thoughts into words. Yes, I am a bit like her in that respect... And we have the same eyes too," she added, smiling. "Only mine are prettier, right?"

"Oh, much prettier!" said Dora Rosário warmly. "There's no comparison."

Ernesto went to the Museum on the day Dora Rosário had asked her assistant to go and sell Duarte's stamp collection at a specialty shop nearby. That is why, when Ernesto arrived, she was alone. Or, more specifically, she was standing in front of a small Venetian mirror applying some lipstick, something he could never have imagined the Salvation Army Dora Rosário doing. As I mentioned, the antediluvian Dora had disliked him. Ernesto was quite rich, and his name often appeared in the newspapers regarding some board or other of which he was chair. However, she was not the sort to make unnecessary comments about this person or that, about Ernesto for example. After that one allusion to his smugness, she occasionally smiled elliptically at something I said, but nothing more—enough, though, for me to understand (more or less) what she thought of him. A man convinced of his own importance. The sort who doesn't just go somewhere, he proceeds; who doesn't speak, he opines; who doesn't just read a document, he immerses himself in it. That sort. The worst thing is, she was right. Although whether she did actually think this, I can't be sure. It's mere supposition, like so much else.

I've often wondered—now that my time is my own—what could have led Dora to take the attitude she took. Posthumous revenge? A desire to make up for lost time? Or both, who knows? In my opinion (which will, in this context, be hers), love had nothing to do with it, and Ernesto was simply the first man Dora met following *the late-night conversation with her mother-in-law*. Because even when filled with the modest desire to live life to the fullest that had suddenly (yet somehow gradually) taken hold of her, Dora was not the kind of person to befriend or even chat with someone who came into the shop and asked the price of writing desk X or picture Y. As I have said more than once, she was a woman of few words, and, although, during the days that followed she may have said a little too much, like someone who's drunk, the truth is she wasn't one to waste her breath. You might object that she and I were friends, but, as I think I've made abundantly clear, she and her daughter were on one side and the rest of the world was on the other. What's more, she understood the word "friend" in its most basic sense. That of two women with relatively little to do, who occasionally talk about this and that in order to pass the time. Perhaps she was right and that was all our friendship amounted to. Not that I had ever said a word against Duarte, whom I had never actually met. And even if I had said anything, by the time Ernesto visited the Museum, the image of Duarte had almost completely faded away, and he was no longer a topic of conversation.

Anyway, Ernesto went into the shop, saw a woman applying her makeup, and asked if Senhora Dona Dora was around.

Knowing Ernesto as I do, I'm beginning to doubt that, when he took a closer look, he really didn't recognize her, but the fact is, she was completely taken in and felt genuinely flattered. Flattered and grateful, obviously. He must have seemed to her a very pleasant fellow, worthy of her esteem. Pleasant and estimable in equal parts. Well, half-pleasant and half-estimable, both qualities in perfect balance. Such a response is only human. And women, however intelligent, are particularly susceptible to praise, even praise by omission, even the most sensible of women, as Dora Rosário was at the time.

"It's Dr. Ernesto Laje, isn't it?" she asked, smiling broadly. And she held out her hand. "How are you?"

I can see her emerging from among the dusty lamps and bibelots as if from her own ashes, brandishing her new smile, all bright pink and brilliant white, because she's always had nice teeth. A tug at her tight skirt, another, rather artificial, primp of her perfectly coiffed hair, with little bangs to conceal her rather too high forehead, the gesture of a bad actress in a bad play, and a sudden look of *je suis à vous, cher ami.* I wouldn't say she turned on the charm, but she did offer him an opening gambit. How long had it been since they'd met? Let me see…the last time was, was…

"About three years ago."

"Yes, it must be at least that."

"Possibly more."

"Possibly…" She paused. "Time passes…"

It does indeed. Now it was his turn to say

something nice, and Ernesto has never been one to miss an opportunity. Nothing very original, mind, but he probably wasn't trying to be. I mean, he didn't try too hard. However old hat, it would all be new to Dora Rosário. "Well, it doesn't seem to have passed for you at all." Or something along those lines.

She no doubt blushed with pleasure. "What hasn't passed?" she asked, probably just to be sure.

"Time. Why, when I last saw you…" He was possibly about to say that she had appeared much older then, but he stopped himself. "You're looking really well," he said instead, gazing at her with that all-embracing gaze, which not only touches people, it covers them, wraps around them, cuts them off from wherever they were before he looked at them, takes their breath away, if you like. "You've grown younger," he said at last, confident now of the power of his gaze. "And in the most delightful way."

Dora Rosário seemed slightly melancholy. "I thought that life…" she began, then appeared to forget what it was she was about to say. However, she immediately smiled again, like someone choosing to override some painful subject. "So, you're interested in that rug, is that right?

You're in luck. A German lady also expressed interest, but she never came back." She took a few steps toward the rug, and Ernesto saw for the first time that she was very elegantly dressed. Dora touched the rug with her hand. "Here it is. Apparently, these are precisely the colors you were looking for…"

He said: "They are indeed. It's a really beautiful rug."

"Woven by Bakhtiari nomads, southwest of Isfahan," she said, like a guard in a public museum.

"You mean, Princess Soraya and all that?" said Ernesto.

"Exactly. As you see, it's divided into squares, each with a theme: birds, trees, especially cedar trees, the tree of life."

"The tree of life, eh? For us it's the tree of death, although in Mediterranean countries…"

"It also has some inscriptions in Persian."

"What do they say?"

"Ah, as to that…they may perhaps speak of prosperity, long life, love, the usual things. In a word, happiness."

She didn't mention my name, didn't refer to me at all. She didn't say that the last time they had met had been at my house, when she'd come to ask me for the address of an English tutor I'd told her about earlier, because the one they had was apparently not very cultured and certainly not good enough for her precious Lisa. She didn't say that I had been the one who told her that the colors of the rug were exactly what Dr. Ernesto Laje was looking for (now that he was furnishing his house in Sintra). Obviously, I can't swear that this *is* what happened, but it would suit me if it was.

He asked her for the price, and she told him. It was cheaper because, as he could see, it was secondhand. Otherwise…ten *contos*. A steal, to use the language of commerce. Ernesto said that he would think about it and asked if she could wait two days for an answer. He needed to go back to Sintra (because the rug was for his house in Sintra) to check that it was the right size. "It's nine by twelve, isn't it?" he asked.

"Nine by twelve and a half."

"So I can come back in two days' time, certain that it won't have been sold…"

"Of course."

Ernesto left, after giving her a firm handshake and another of those cocooning gazes. That night, he and I ate supper again at the Choupana, and I asked: "Have you spoken to Dora?"

"Which Dora?"

"Dora Rosário."

"Ah, Dora Rosário. Yes, I have. By the way, what the hell has happened to her?"

I, of course, didn't understand what he meant, because I had not yet seen her in her new skin.

Aunt Júlia used to dream about flying saucers, and that was one of the absurd reasons Dora had always felt closer to her than to her mother-in-law. Lisa would sometimes stay over at her grandmother's place on a Saturday night, and when she did, she would sleep on a divan in her aunt's bedroom. In the morning, her aunt would tell her about that night's dream or some other dream she'd had some other night. "You'll laugh," she would say. "You really will." Her dreams were never particularly varied, but they were very detailed, almost frighteningly so. "A segment of a sphere, not illuminated, you understand, but luminous. I mean, it was made entirely of light in the way the sea is made of water and the earth of dirt. It was sitting very still, the sphere, or rather, the segment of a sphere, the disc, in the middle of a deserted beach or a

deserted road." She was walking or running, getting closer and closer, but she didn't feel in the
least afraid, as if it was as normal as running for
a bus. And yet, at the same time, it felt as if she
was walking or running in place, not moving or
only very little. "Ages ago now, I saw a movie
called *Owl River*. And that's what it was like. I
kept reaching out, trying to touch it, but I never
made it." It was really exhausting. Just as she was
about to touch it, when she *knew* she was about
to touch it, the segment would start moving
away. "Isn't that funny?" she always asked at the
end, looking hard at her niece. One morning,
she gave an unexpectedly sly little smile and said:
"One of these nights, I'll catch it up and then
you'll never see me again," adding: "Oh, how I
wish I could reach that sphere!"

"Aunt Júlia's a bit crazy, isn't she?" Lisa asked
her mother after one such evening, just before
going to bed, although her questions were never
what you could really call questions. They were
more like thoughts spoken out loud, but in an
interrogative tone that invited whomever she
was with to join in.

"Crazy? That's a bit simplistic," said Dora
Rosário. "Sticking labels on people is a bad habit,

pinning them to some spot where we think they belong, like butterflies in a collection. Good and bad, crazy and sane... As if it were possible to categorize someone like that! There are so many stopping places along a continuum, thousands of them. Where would you and I be on that continuum, for example? I really don't know, but certainly not at either of the extremes."

"You would be."

"Me?" Dora said with a shrug, feeling slightly put out. "No, not even me. Not even me, Lisa."

"Yes, perhaps you're right," agreed Lisa. "Anyone who's a bit out of the ordinary...like Aunt Júlia..."

"Poor Aunt Júlia."

The conversation went no further, but that night, Dora Rosário spent some time thinking about herself, about Duarte's name (his image having almost gone, now that she no longer summoned it up), and about Aunt Júlia. She didn't think about Ernesto Laje. Either deliberately or because he wasn't yet a strong enough presence to impose himself on her thoughts. Anyway, the fact is that she didn't think about him—she herself told me so.

I can't now remember why she talked to me

about Aunt Júlia and her dreams, but I suppose there must have been a reason. It was definitely apropos of something or other. Perhaps she'd spoken to Ernesto about flying saucers or about Aunt Júlia, when, two days later, he'd returned to the Museum. I really don't know.

Ernesto arrived, spoke to Dora, and sat down for a while to study the rug. It really was a beauty. It was rather like a mural with its luscious old golds and slightly greenish midnight blues. "The size is perfect," he said. And he added that he really loved old things, although our day and age was probably better suited to simple furniture, plain rugs, and big windows open onto the world.

"Functional designs," she said, also sitting down, tugging at her skirt, which was now shorter and tighter.

"Yes, functional designs. I think 'functional' works really well in offices or places of business. Yes, for a work environment, that's fine. Not at home though. It's not comforting enough somehow." Then he said: "Listen, why don't we get a bite to eat and talk about furniture. I need some more pieces, and you might be able to help."

Since this was work-related—or so she told

herself—she said: "Yes, why not?" in her newly acquired nonchalant style, before turning to her assistant and giving him a few instructions. Then she put on her jacket and said, smiling: "Shall we go?"

They went. In his car, one of his cars, the most luxurious—why the most luxurious?—the DS. "How about going to Cascais?"

"Isn't that rather far?" she said vaguely. "I have to be back by seven o'clock."

"What do you mean 'far'? We'll be there in thirty minutes. We can have a bite to eat and come straight back. I have to be in my office by six. Some terrible old bore is coming to see me, and I have to put up with him because I need him."

"How about going to Estoril?" he had said to me one day, years ago. He didn't have the DS then, and had to make do with a Volkswagen, which, at the time, I thought resembled a big stupid face with mouth, nose, and even two eyes. One of the early models. Later, he swapped it for a small, restless cyclops, with one large eye in the middle of its forehead. And, of course, off I'd gone in his old-fashioned Volkswagen. Where will I go now that I'm forty-five? There are some escape routes, which I've already considered. Good works. Drinking alone, getting drunk alone, all very degrading, but still… Other women go into a frenzy of knitting, as if they want to knit together the threads of their life. Others turn to poetry or religion. None of those things tempt me. But I'm not here to talk about myself.

"Life isn't all roses," said Ernesto, still talking about the client he had to see.

And he was saying this to Dora of all people! Dora felt herself tense up a little, and was almost tempted to say something disagreeable to this man who was, after all, a somewhat unpleasant poseur. She said nothing though. Suddenly, she realized that she couldn't say anything, it was impossible. And this troubled her. Dora Rosário was a calm woman, and always had been. And she still was. It was then—I remember now—that she made some comment about possible ways of escaping from life, a life that definitely wasn't all roses. And she talked about Aunt Júlia and her flying saucers and the conversations she had while asleep. Not a word about her hysterical attacks though.

Then, laughing, Ernesto asked if Dora believed in flying saucers too, and she said that she didn't, but rather regretted not being able to. She had believed in fairies and the Baby Jesus until quite late, and then, when they departed, she'd felt rather lost. If flying saucers could come and fill that vacuum, she would receive them with open arms. Alas, though, she didn't believe in them, which revealed something like a lack of faith. But what could she do?

"But your aunt really does believe in them?"

"She's my husband's aunt actually," Dora said. "But, yes, she does, and good for her."

"Why?"

"Because at least she believes in something."

"And you don't?"

"Me?"

"Yes, you."

She gave a little laugh. "I believed in my husband," she said, growing suddenly serious again. "But he died once and then died again. After two deaths, there was nothing left. Or very little. So there's nothing left to believe in. And I didn't have a religious upbringing either. I've just focused all my energies on myself and on Lisa…"

"Lisa?"

"My daughter. I don't really care about anyone else. About other people."

Ernesto turned to look at her: "You need to shake off that apathy," he said with feeling. A rather tired old statement, of the kind Dora had heard dozens of times—a handy phrase for both the person saying it and the person hearing it. Said by him, though, in that low caressing voice, it took on a different, almost physical meaning.

"I'm trying to—as you may have noticed," she said, blushing a little.

Ernesto had noticed. "What the hell *did* happen to you?" Dora, however, immediately retreated: "I'm sorry, I don't usually talk about myself…tell my story, I mean," adding: "I keep it all safely locked away."

"You tell it to yourself, which comes to the same thing. You belong to the category of self-talkers, who sometimes get so caught up in their own inner conversation that they don't even hear what other people are saying. They don't even notice life passing them by."

"It already has," she said.

"But you've woken up in time."

Had she really? In time for what, though? To sleep with this man? She shrugged noncommittally. The DS continued swiftly, imperturbably, along the coast road, as if it were flying. Sixty, seventy;

the needle stopped at seventy-five. Ernesto was silent now, his eyes fixed on the road. The light seemed to stitch a line around his profile, which stood out against the blue of the river where it met the sea. Large nose, strong jaw, thin lips. Was he naturally dark or was that a tan? His presence, even when silent, thought Dora, evoked descriptions or slogans along the lines of "Time Is Money," "The Self-Made Man," "The Struggle for Life," and so on.

They arrived and sat down at a table on the terrace of the Restaurante Baía. Ernesto summoned the waiter, or, rather, demanded his presence with a mere lift of his chin, like a man accustomed to making demands for which he was prepared to pay generously. "What would you like to drink?" he asked. "I'll have a whisky, of course." Of course. She would not. Of course.

"Could I have a tea and some toast."

"A slice of cake?" he suggested.

"No, I don't like cake. Toast will be fine."

When the waiter left, Ernesto bestowed his all-embracing gaze on her and said: "So tell me what happened to Father Christmas."

"It wasn't Father Christmas, it was the Baby Jesus," she responded, laughing.

"All right, tell me about him, then. People who talk a lot to themselves have that advantage, they don't get distracted. You remember—which is amazing in itself—that you really missed the fairies and the Baby Jesus, when you were just... how old were you?"

"Eight," she said unhesitatingly, like someone who has recently given long consideration to the matter.

"Eight," said Ernesto. "I wonder what I was thinking about when I was eight? And when you lost them, what did you do?" he asked, not like someone making conversation, but like someone who really needs to know.

Dora gave a faint smile and thought for a moment. "Well," she said, "when I was sick—and I was often sick as a child—there was a ray of sunlight that used to fall across the green quilt on my bed. The ray of light was filled with bright dust motes. For me it was the Milky Way with all its stars. However much the grown-ups insisted that the stars don't move, I refused to believe them. My stars moved all the time, crisscrossing each other, leaving the Milky Way whenever they wanted to. I also enjoyed imagining tiny little men rushing around in my quilt forest, and a princess being pursued. The princess would run away and her pursuers never tired of pursuing her. It was always in my power (the power of my legs, that is) to cause an earthquake. I had tremendous fun when I was sick."

"So I see," he said.

"Then, little by little, I started to find myself. Later, Duarte appeared. And then he disappeared. I did my best to hold on to his image, his memory. I tried so hard, but that meant being constantly alert, never getting distracted. And in the end, I did get distracted. I had no choice."

"Is that why you used to dress like that, so as not to get distracted? It didn't come naturally, I mean."

"No, it didn't come naturally." She gave another brief laugh, not knowing how else to respond, then added, "People find such an attitude strange, but as soon as we abandon it, they start to criticize us."

He drank his whisky, she her tea, and they talked a little about the weather, too hot for the time of year. Ernesto hated the heat. "My house in Sintra is wonderful in that respect," he said. "Not that it's anything extraordinary, it's just a house in the hills, which I bought for a song about twelve years ago. It has a lovely view, though, and I'm thinking of having a swimming pool put in."

"Are you going to live there, then?" asked Dora Rosário, somewhat surprised. And she must immediately have thought: *Manuela's never going to agree to that... I can't see her spending all year up in the hills...* Neither can I. And I've told him so often enough. I'm not the kind of woman to bury herself in the countryside.

"I'm not sure," he said. "Possibly, one day. I did buy it with that idea in mind, an oasis of calm in my hectic life."

The Contest of Life, Time Is Money, etc. "Of course," she said. "It must be lovely."

Then they got up and drove back. On the way, Ernesto told her more about the house. And when they said goodbye, once he'd written her a check and given her a card with his Lisbon address where the rug should be delivered, it was agreed, although neither of them made any explicit arrangement, that one day soon he would drop by the Museum and take her to see his Sintra house. Everything leads me to believe that, even then, my name was never mentioned by either of them.

That night or some other night, but certainly before they visited the house in the hills—again in
the DS—she may have woken in the early hours
and turned on the light, only to be confronted,
almost aggressively, by the three mirrors on her
dressing table, three vague, fluctuating images
that seemed slightly unsettled by the abrupt
change in her appearance. Was that her? Could
it be? The short hair, rumpled by sleep, the eyebrows once thick and now tweezed thin, gave
her an almost wild, startled look. Was that her?
Could it be? In the light of the sand-colored
planet she didn't immediately recognize herself
and drew back slightly. Those three strange vis-
ages—the one in the middle full face, the other
two three-quarter view and back to front—
seemed completely out of place in Dora's bedroom, in Lisa's mother's room, in the widow of

Duarte Rosário's room, and they, too, drew back slightly in alarm. Then Dora once more slipped back into her new skin and became Dora Rosário again, the very same, despite the short hair, the tweezed eyebrows, and the eyes still accentuated by a trace of liner, and despite her having let go of Duarte's dull image, she sat resolutely up in bed and began thinking. This was an old habit of hers, regardless. If thoughts crowded in on her while she was at work or in between tasks, she would put them to the side. If some important or even grave thought occurred to her then, she would say to herself: I'll think about that later (preferably at night). And so she would do her thinking when the rest of the household was sleeping, and it seemed to her that she could think more freely when alone, with no fear that her thinking would be interrupted or intruded upon. She could happily expand on her thoughts then, like a radio tower working away on its own, which meant she could express herself more clearly on one particular wavelength.

That night, she picked up her husband's photo, which she kept on her bedside table because of Lisa, and she studied it for a long time. She had been in the habit of doing this, but for different reasons. Before that late-night conversation with Ana, she used to try and fill herself with his image, to summon up his presence, to give sustenance to his ever more fragile life. Because death is only complete when memories die. However, never before had she looked at him for so long or so keenly as she did that night. Or so coolly. And never before had he seemed to her so empty, so dull, so paper-thin. A photo fit for a gravestone, she thought. One of those graves surrounded by faded artificial flowers. A bit of old paper, nothing more.

At first, in the early years following his death, he would still answer when she called, he would smile at her and say things. And Dora would feel comforted. But even those smiles, those words, that comfort were all her own creation. An invention. There was another woman in the city at whom he smiled more sweetly, to whom he said more things. Little by little, then, the smiles had grown feebler, vaguer, the words almost inaudible, the image just a pale smudge whose deficiencies she struggled hard to justify. Yet even so, Dora had persevered, not wanting to understand, to admit, that Duarte was merely a point of reference in her conversations: so-and-so happened

X number of years or months before Duarte died
or after Duarte died. He was also an example.
She spoke of his kindness, his purity, his lack of
ambition or of any desire to emulate others, and
then she would say or think: Duarte. Sometimes
she didn't even need to say his name or think it—
he would come, would appear automatically. But
that, too, became rarer over time. Not because he
was overtaken by more exciting examples. The
truth is that purity, kindness, lack of ambition or
the desire to emulate others had lost their former
status as fundamental virtues. Other qualities had
arisen that were equally worthy of her admiration (or of her distrust, a mixture of admiration
and distrust). The ability to know things, which
Lisa appeared to have; more than that, her ability
to know what was best, what best suited her. Her
intelligence. Her beauty. Her love of life. The
extraordinary facility she had for making friends.

"She's my one consolation," her mother-
in-law would say, gazing adoringly at Lisa, and
adding, like someone recognizing certain atavis-
tic qualities: "She's going to achieve everything
I failed to achieve, succeed where I failed. I look
at her and I feel I'm not about to die just yet,
I'm going to hang around for a few more years

because I have things to do, to achieve." Lisa would laugh out loud and run over to her and kiss her. "Oh really, Ana!" she would exclaim, then perform a graceful pirouette before heading off to her room to study English. She had already decided. She was going to be an airline stewardess, but she could only apply when she was eighteen. How irritating was that?

Dora Rosário suddenly felt cold and so put a shawl around her shoulders while she continued to think. She was thinking, for example, about why the thing her mother-in-law had told her during that memorable late-night conversation, hadn't really upset her that much, but had instead been a weight off her mind. Like someone who feels too hot in bed and throws off the blankets. First, there's an almost intense feeling of cold, but you soon get used to it. And insofar as it was possible, she *had* grown used to that knowledge. She didn't hate Duarte for having loved another woman. It was perfectly possible that he *had* grown bored with her company. Something Ana had said one day ages ago came into her head: "I don't think that's what he needed." She may have been right, and maybe he had found Dora boring because she always agreed with him, even

when she didn't actually share his views. She
was the person she hated, and still did, for being so stupid—herself, not Duarte or anyone else.
Duarte and his mother had done what people do.
They had, each in their own way, been human.
Whether they had been good or bad didn't matter. Whereas she…

Some people got religion or killed themselves after losing someone, whether that person
died or just left them. Dora Rosário, however,
didn't blame anyone else for her misfortune.
Only herself. She loathed herself, but not enough
to seek relief in death. No, she simply disliked
herself, a more modest sentiment. And when, for
example, she was standing before the mirror to
apply her lipstick at the very moment Ernesto
Laje came into the shop, doing so had given her
no pleasure; indeed, what she felt was a degree of
discreet rage.

This was the image of Ernesto that came
into her mind that night. Him entering the
Museum for the first time and asking if Senhora
Dora had left. She put her husband's photo down
on the bedside table and took a long, hard, un-
flinching look at her mental image of Ernesto
Laje. What was he doing there? His face was

fairly unremarkable. Slightly lined, with strong features, dark eyes, and a frank smile. It was, though, a lively face, there was life in those eyes and that smile. He was accompanied, too, by a perfume that was hard to pin down. Cologne? Shaving cream? Aftershave? One of those things that living men use. There was, above all, that all-embracing gaze, for she had forgotten that men still looked at women in that way.

Ernesto was giving her the same all-embracing gaze that night, when she was the only one awake in her household, and Dora allowed herself to dwell in that gaze and feel how pleasant it was. She also thought of me, although only in passing, because as I said, I was just one of the vast legion of *others*. Indeed, the only reason she paused to think about me was because I had entered her head alongside Ernesto. Perhaps, in a way, I am to blame for Dora Rosário's attitude. One day, when I was talking to her about me and him (a silent, solitary woman is a real find as a confidante), I told her certain things, and even though this was some years ago now, still today I regret having done so. I said, for example, that with the passing of time, I had ceased to be his companion and become, instead, the landscape to which he had grown accustomed, though if that landscape suddenly went up in flames, he would be most alarmed. Only if it had gone up in flames of its own accord, I explained, not if he had set fire to it. But landscapes tend not to go up in flames or disappear into some seismic fault-line, a thing so rare that, when it occurs, it makes the headlines. What does happen is that the person in question grows tired of the landscape, not because he has found another more alluring one (nobody exchanges one landscape for another), but because he has met someone who fills him with disdain for all other possible landscapes. That is what I once said to Dora. And as further proof of my unease, I said that he had even occasionally commented that he liked tall women (*forgetting* that I was short), and blonde women (*forgetting* that I had dark hair). *Forgetting*, I repeat. He was incapable of being willfully cruel or even discourteous.

On that day, Dora asked me with an evident lack of interest: "Do you think there *is* someone else?"

I laughed at such ingenuousness. "Is there someone else?" There was always someone else, I mean, almost always. It was simply that no one had yet turned up with sufficient oomph to make him abandon the landscape he was used to. A very tranquil landscape, with no storms. He likes fine weather and easy walks. Besides, I'm not the jealous type. I think jealousy is a pointless, destructive emotion. More than that, it's an emotion from which no one emerges a winner. He's not the jealous type either, although in his case it's different. He never needed to be jealous, because I was never interested in anyone else.

"What if you had been?" asked Dora rather daringly.

"I don't know. I'd have to think about that. However, since the problem has never arisen, there's no point in inventing hypotheses. I really do love Ernesto."

"You speak as if..."

"I speak as I feel. I don't do dramas. They make me break out in a rash. It's not a role I could ever play."

Then Dora Rosário must have thought: "Manuela won't mind. Besides, she'll never find out, because nobody's going to take him from her landscape." She knew her limitations, and was perfectly aware that a new hairstyle, a touch of lipstick, and a more fashionable suit weren't enough to turn her into a femme fatale. She also knew that she was already thirty-six, had never been either pretty or ugly, that her cloistered existence spent in the company of rare antiques and memories of Duarte had removed her from life, and that it would be very hard for her to readjust to a different existence. During that retreat, which one couldn't even describe as spiritual, she had read very little, had entirely given up going to plays, and had, for good reason, lost touch with almost all her female friends (with whom she'd fallen out) and her husband's friends (whom she had all too often asked for money). Her thoughts were, therefore, limited to her daughter and, by force of circumstance, her mother-in-law and Aunt Júlia. Apart from that and the antiques, she had nothing much else to talk about.

So why had Ernesto invited her to go to Cascais and why had he looked at her like that? There lay a problem she would prefer not to probe too deeply. It was simply a matter of time. And she enjoyed his company. It was a bit like being a girl again and having some nice boy she knew follow her in the street. It was best just to wait and see what happened. He'd said he would call her to arrange a trip to Sintra "so that she could give him advice about some furniture he was thinking of buying." *What if she made some excuse?* she thought, again picking up Duarte's photo—it looked even duller than before, a dead photograph. All that was left of him, because everything else... His soul, if he had one, was far away; and as for his body...she didn't even want to think about that.

At first, Dora's lack of interest in such matters had infuriated her mother-in-law. Indeed, it had been almost the only source of friction between them. Because Ana—who didn't believe in God or the Devil—went every Sunday to take flowers to her son's grave nevertheless, and made every effort to keep the gravestone clean and the flowers she had planted around it watered, as if these were proof of the saintliness of the person lying there—always assuming he *was* there. She worked hard on that little artificial garden, even placing some flowerpots on the gravestone, paying the sexton to look after the plot, and, in conversation with Dora, would sometimes dangle her bait: "You never go to the cemetery, so you've no idea how huge the place is." Dora Rosário would smile faintly and concentrate on her food, since those conversations usually occurred over supper on Sunday. "Really?" Dora would say.

"Yes, huge. You should go there sometime, just to see." Just to see.

One day, Dora had said to her: "The photo I have in my bedroom is more Duarte than those dried-up bones you place flowers on."

Ana's flabby bosom had trembled with indignation. "How can you talk like that? How can you say such things in front of his mother and his daughter?"

Lisa had immediately shrugged indifferently. "Oh, don't worry about me..." She was ten at the time.

Her grandmother ignored her. She was quite worked up, which she very rarely was. "Who will tend his grave when I die?" she said. "Actually, I've been thinking of buying a family vault, which would avoid such problems. Duarte, José, Aunt Júlia, and I won't need anyone to look after us then. And as for Lisa, many, many years from now..."

Dora Rosário was thus excluded, rejected even before she had entered the Rosário family's future residence, built in a wealthy part of town. *For fear of cheapening it*, she thought. Even after death, they want to have their solid house, with respectable people as neighbors, so they can play an eternal game of canasta in a house full of nothing but dried flowers. Full, too, of worms, of course, but her mother-in-law preferred not to think about that, perhaps because her turn to provide the feast was fast approaching and she could feel it coming. That's why she looked to her granddaughter and consoled herself with the thought that Lisa would still be around to arrange things.

Dora took off her shawl, folded it up neatly, then turned out the light. Before going to sleep, however, she wondered if Ernesto would call her the next day.

He did call, and they arranged that he would come and pick her up on Sunday, right after lunch. That night, Dora Rosário told her daughter that she would be going out on Sunday afternoon and might not be back in time for supper at Ana's. Would she mind going on her own? Lisa snorted. Why ever would she mind? Then she grew serious and asked: "Are you planning to get married again?"

This left Dora feeling perplexed. "Me?" she said. "Me?" she repeated. "Whoever put that idea in your head?"

Lisa shrugged: "You obviously don't have a very high opinion of me, Mom. Do you really think I need other people to put ideas in my head?"

"No, but..." Dora gave her a rather clumsy kiss, partly so that Lisa wouldn't see her face.

"Nothing could be further from my mind, and besides, there isn't even anyone I like," she said in a very earnest voice.

Lisa gave one of her loud laughs: "You talk as if it would be a problem for me. I hardly knew Dad, and I certainly don't think of him as the very pinnacle of perfection. Actually, I'd rather like you to get married. When single women reach a certain age, they're so…frightening. They wither away, don't they? One of the reasons I like Aunt Júlia is that she hasn't withered away, she dreams of flying saucers."

"That's just an escape from reality."

"She's up-to-date though," said Lisa. "She's a modern woman, embracing science fiction. Dad was really fond of her, wasn't he? Fonder than he was of Ana perhaps?"

"Ana was his mother, Lisa. He was always very fond of her."

"Tell me about Dad."

This request could not have come at a worse moment, and Dora even wondered if there was some particular reason why Lisa was asking that question then. But no, Lisa's gaze was attentive and transparent, her small mouth serious.

"Your father was a very good man," Dora

said. "Not an ounce of ambition…" She hesitated, because suddenly she couldn't think quite what Duarte's other qualities had been.

"*I'm* ambitious," said Lisa. "I take after my grandmother. I would have preferred to take after you, but here we are. Besides, ambition can be a good quality."

"It can, that's true, but your father didn't think so. Well, we all have a right to our own opinions, don't we? And your father…"

Lisa, however, had other things to do and was no longer interested in hearing about her father. It was half past five, and her German tutor was about to arrive. "I have to go," she said, yawning slightly.

Through the glass, the sun failed to bring any comfort. A thin veil, barely touching her skin, could not prevent the shudder provoked by the damp mountain air whirling around inside the car. Dora Rosário had her hands on her lap. They were large, bony hands, and the skin around her fingers was already growing wrinkled (when did that happen? And how strange that she had only just noticed); hands that were numb with cold, even though it was spring, hands that the cold seemed to have suddenly made still thinner. Her ring, the only one the pawnbrokers had not yet gotten from her—a band of gold set with an aquamarine—was suddenly too big for her, as if it didn't belong to her. She shivered, and Ernesto broke the silence to ask if she was feeling all right. "Yes, fine," said Dora, laughing for no reason. "I'm just a bit cold," she added, "which is great—a sign that I'm still alive." Then, eyeing the madly flickering needle on the speedometer: "Are we nearly there?"

He, however, was looking straight ahead, as if concentrating entirely on the white line down the middle of the road. It was growing colder, and the wind was ruffling their hair. He remained serious, as if he wasn't even there. Where was he? And with whom? Who, put simply, was he thinking about?

As she herself told me, it suddenly occurred to her, right there in the middle of the hills, that she was waiting for him to say something along the lines of: "One day, a person meets another person and thinks: this is the one. It's not a matter of love at first sight. It's just a realization. This is the one. And you are the one, Dora Rosário. We could have met sooner, but we still have time, don't we?"

Instead, he talked to her about the large room that he intended to have as his living room. What furniture would she suggest? Disparate pieces, of course, but not so disparate that they clashed. Dora Rosário began making suggestions, and did so until the car stopped.

I won't go into what, for me, are unpleasant details. I won't make any suppositions in this chapter. And Dora was extremely discreet. She didn't describe (nor did she need to) the almost empty house or that particular room, which wasn't in the least surprised to see what it was seeing, having already seen so much. She only said that afterward, *afterward,* she opened the window that looks out over the small, still-empty pond, the future swimming pool of Ernesto's dreams (now almost finished I'm told), and asked him (without turning around, still gazing out at the pond), "Why?" Just that: "Why?" He took a while to respond, and Dora thought it was because he didn't know quite how to answer. Poor innocent Dora. As if Ernesto had ever been caught napping. Ernesto with no answer cocked and ready? Don't make me laugh. There could have been various reasons to explain that delay. To start with, a feeling that it wasn't worth wasting his deathless prose on her. Hesitating between various reasons, all too blunt to offer her just then. Not even having the courage to choose the simplest of all, the most hackneyed and least true: that he loved her. From the little he knew of Dora Rosário, he was sure she wouldn't believe him if he came out with such a whopping great lie.

For a while, he said nothing, then he did speak to her about me. Yes, about me, when—without turning around to look at him—she had asked him "Why?" At first, I didn't understand what I had to do with that whole mess, but when Dora Rosário told me what Ernesto had said, I had to admire his sheer chutzpah. Amazing. "I'm not happy," he said. "Not at all happy. I really love Manuela, but that's precisely why I'm not happy, and—if you'll forgive my frankness—why I'm always looking around here and there for a little excitement."

That "here and there" exactly described their "relationship," a chance encounter with no complications; or, rather, whose complications he rejected right from the start. Was this his usual method? Possibly, although I'm not convinced he was in the habit of dotting the *i*'s quite so early on. This was possibly because none of his previous visitors had ever asked him "Why" so frankly, so bluntly, straight out like that.

And when, having tired of the pond once and for all, she did turn to look at him, Ernesto plunged into the confused and tragic tale of a childless couple and his own sadness at having no children. He, Ernesto Laje, was a fighter, but he wanted to know what or whom he was fighting for. The truth is, it had never really bothered me, not having children, I mean. And would it have changed things if it had, I wonder. He, however, was bent on making a tragedy out of the situation. Then he spoke about his niece, his one remaining relative, an ambitious little hypocrite, who was always telling everyone (anyone who would be sure to pass it on to him) that she didn't even like going to Uncle Ernesto's house, because people might think she was after his money; if he'd been poor, yes, she'd go then, of course, but certainly not the way things were. That's what the dear child was like. A real sweetie. He no longer thought about it, about having children, that is, well…he was forty-two now. It would be too late anyway. He would die before they reached adulthood or be old. It was an insoluble problem, but a problem nonetheless.

It seemed to me that the name of the problem wasn't Manuela, but he'd found a way of *making* me the problem. He was unhappy because I'd failed to bear him any children, so he was obliged to look for compensations elsewhere. On the other hand, he really did love me and wouldn't change me for the world. A very vicious, vicious circle. As I said, I'm not the dramatic type, which is why I've always understood that, on the one hand, he was basically right (in fact, when I met him, he was more or less engaged to a young Englishwoman who would certainly have given him a few pink, chubby, towheaded children with no visible eyebrows just like their mother… lovely Anglo-Portuguese babies); on the other hand, if he had had children, he would have been obliged to invent another alibi (the deep bond with his children, of course!).

I've always thought his longing for children was rather cerebral. What Ernesto likes most of all (and what gives him, I think, an almost physical pleasure) is earning money, and to that end he pours all his intelligence and his infallibility into the skillful disquisitions on which depend the present and the future of two men: the one who has the money to pay him, and the one who doesn't. It just so happens that the one who doesn't have the money is usually in the right, but that's a minor matter. Yes, he likes to have money to spend, but mainly he likes hoarding it away. It's important to remember that he's a self-made man and came from humble beginnings. But why hoard it away? For whom? That's where the problem of the nonexistent children arose, and the all-too-existent niece. This was why he found consolation—here and there—in the occasional moment of excitement. Excitement? No, not even that. Excitement with Dora Rosário? No way!

If it had ever occurred to me, however remotely, that Dora Rosário would be a problem or would cause a problem...but how could I ever have thought such a thing? Dora and Ernesto? Even if I'd known about it, I would have thought: "It won't last a month. Just let it run its course." As I said, I'm not the jealous type. And I would have laughed just a little at poor Dora's secret dream of love. Because on her part, it would be just that. Only later did I learn precisely what happened, and the consequences. And then I didn't feel like laughing at all. Sitting opposite me, Dora Rosário kept tugging at her skirt, an obsessive gesture acquired since the last time I'd seen her, and she was very loyal. She always was, albeit rather belatedly. I, however, didn't care at all about Dora Rosário's loyalty. I would have laughed in her face if it hadn't been for what happened later. Since she insisted on recounting her entire story, though, I had to hear how she hurriedly got dressed, saying that she had to rush back in time for supper at her mother-in-law's house.

"But I thought we were going to have supper together somewhere."

"No, no, I have to go. I've just remembered something really urgent I have to do. A letter to a foreign client. I need to get it in the post today."

"Fine, we'll go, then. I hope I haven't offended you. I can be a bit…"

He must have been feeling annoyed with himself for having allowed himself to be drawn into confiding things that might have made him look rather ridiculous. Those words, "I'm always looking around here and there for a little excitement," were still stuck in his craw. How stupid, he thought. But then why the hell had she asked "Why"? No one asked such a question at this stage of the game.

When they set off down the winding road back into Sintra, he was feeling absolutely furious with himself and driving at more than sixty miles an hour. When he hit the tree, he must have been doing nearly ninety. It was a miracle they survived.

Dora Rosário, of course, had passed out, but she insisted on giving me a blow-by-blow account of everything she could remember from the moment she came around. I think I must have looked slightly irritated or bored, but she still didn't spare me a single detail. She was probably too immersed in her own story, a story she was telling for the first time.

She woke up in a very white room, and her whole body hurt. She had bandages on her face and one arm in a cast. She struggled to remember but thought she could recall lying on a hard, unfamiliar bed that kept moving and was surrounded (it must have been) by mysterious men all in white. Life and death are separated only by a knife edge (where had she read that?) and in her sleep, she had been balanced precariously on that edge. What were they talking about? What were they saying? Her body was asleep, but what about her soul, her immortal soul? This was the first time in her life she had thought about her immortal soul. Where had it been, assuming it did exist, given that she could remember nothing?

"Where was my soul, Sister, while they were operating on me? They did operate, didn't they?" she asked the nun who appeared shortly afterward, brandishing a thermometer and a broad smile. She looked at Dora hard, as if distrustful of such innocence. Then she laughed quietly: "What a question!" – "I just wanted to know…" – "To know what?" – "I wanted to know…" Dora said, speaking with some difficulty, because she could barely open her mouth, "…if my soul was anesthetized too." A silence then another laugh: "Anesthetized…no, of course not." – "Are you sure, Sister?" Of course she was sure, how could she not be? Her life was composed of certainties joined one to the other, forming long, unending chains. That's why she could laugh so freely and confidently. "Of course I'm sure." – "Where was it then?" – "Perhaps it was resting, like us when we're asleep." – "Or curled up somewhere, watching and trembling a bit, if it's not a very brave soul, Sister." – "All right, trembling a bit, then." – "Or a lot. I said 'a brave soul,' but that isn't really what I meant. Sometimes bravery… What I meant was either a clean soul or a dirty one." – "Well, in the first instance…" – "Let's say slightly crumpled." – "Crumpled, eh?" – "Yes, like clothes when you've been wearing them for a while." – "I see." No, she didn't see, not that it really mattered. Dora closed her eyes, exhausted by the sheer effort of speaking and having already forgotten what it was that she had asked. Exhausted.

Lisa went to see her, as did Ana and Aunt Júlia, but they didn't stay long, anxious not to tire her out. And she didn't ask them to stay. Because it was just so good to close her eyes and see the clouds.

Spirals and spirals of cone-shaped mountains, covered in smooth, immaculately white snow with no hidden dips, so white it hurt her eyes, or perhaps it would be more accurate to say that the whiteness held her gaze and wouldn't let go. And she, eyes closed, stared and stared. The mountains were very soft and fluffy. It would have been so delicious to fall into them and stay there, suspended between heaven and earth, and forget about everything forever. Suddenly, though, the mountains were no longer mountains. The scene vanished and what she could see were small icebergs adrift in a great cold sea, incredibly serene and transparent, in which were submerged tiny little houses and gray-green forests, which must have swayed with the tides. A pause, and then the clouds were back. Now, though, she was actually in the clouds, rolling around in them, the way she used to play in the sand dunes as a child, shrieking with delight, her mouth full of sand. Her mouth, however—assuming she had one, which was doubtful—was empty and silent. She was gliding downward in slow motion. What had happened to the force of gravity? What about terminal velocity? It was as if she had wings, but no need to open them. She would always arrive unscathed, always stop in time, alighting effortlessly at the foot of the cold mountains. She didn't consider climbing them again. Why bother if she didn't have to? She continued to descend, though, slipping and sliding down the slopes, again and again and again. Where was she coming from? Where was she going?

These were her dreams. There was the sea too, a vast, very calm sea, but a proper sea this time, its waves breaking on immense, deserted beaches. She was swimming in that sea, but it also felt almost as if she were flying; she made slow, easy movements, as if the very blue water were a gentle, maternal element, helping rather than hindering.

"And Ernesto? What could have happened to him?" she wondered when she wasn't dreaming. "What about the other person in the car?" she asked the doctor who came to see her the next day.

"He's absolutely fine, don't worry. He went straight home. He was thrown out of the car and landed in a pile of straw, or a pile of something, and all he did was sprain his wrist." He added: "Dr. Laje has phoned to ask how you are. He's just devastated by what happened. Devastated."

"Oh really!" she said.

So he was devastated, was he? Devastated. She would have laughed, if she could laugh, if that were physically possible, but, at the time, dressings and bandages—and the wounds themselves, of course—prevented her from doing so. Devastated. And what was she? Sick and devastated and utterly ashamed. "I'm always looking around here and there for a little excitement." But what did she expect? Was she actually in love with Ernesto Laje? No, but that didn't stop her from feeling deeply hurt. Rather as if she'd been slapped in the face. Devastated. Was he perhaps concerned that she might sue him for damages? Was that what he thought?

Dora Rosário misjudged him. A week later, as soon as he could go out (because he had been badly bruised), he proved extremely thoughtful and efficient. He didn't just call her apartment to ask if there was anything he could do to be useful. He went there, before supper, and asked to speak to some family member about the accident. "Miss!" bawled the maid, who was not in the habit of receiving visitors. Lisa appeared, or rather, materialized before him, face flushed from trying to perfect a pirouette. She was all black tights, fair hair, and golden eyes.

"Are you Senhora Dora's daughter?" he asked in amazement.

"I am. Do come in." And she preceded him into the living room. "Do have a seat. My mother's in the hospital, I've just come from there…"

"I know. Your mother was in my car. I'd asked her to give me some advice on furnishing my house in Sintra, and she was kind enough to go with me."

"Oh, so it was you," Lisa said, looking at him intently. "Weren't you injured at all?"

"Well, I sprained my wrist. I'm just naturally lucky, I suppose; I landed on a pile of soft dirt someone happened to leave there. I had some slight bruising to my shoulder and my leg, but nothing serious."

"Good for you," she said.

"I was like a bullet fired at a target. I hit the bull's-eye."

"I meant good for you being naturally lucky. I think I am too. That's a good thing."

"It is," he said. "Very good."

He sat down. So did she, on the other side of the room. "It's really reassuring," he went on. "Even when things don't seem to be going particularly well, it all works out splendidly in the end."

"I'm still very young," she said. "I just turned seventeen a month ago. And yet..."

"Is that all?" asked Ernesto, interrupting her. "I would have thought you were easily eighteen, or even nineteen."

Lisa smiled, delighted. "Seriously?" she asked. "When I'm eighteen..." She opened wide her slender, black leotard-clad arms and elegantly flapped her wings: "Paris...London...New

York…Berlin…perhaps the Far East…Africa…
It'll be so exciting."

"You want to be a stewardess, then?"

She tilted her head to one side. "Exactly."
Her thick, luxuriant hair fell like a silken cascade
onto her narrow left shoulder, almost reaching
her sharp left elbow.

"Oh, just the thought of it…" She closed her
eyes, and the light vanished. She was smiling,
though, and her smile was also a sight very much
worth seeing.

I heard this part of the story from Ernesto
himself, who was trying—for the first time—to
be completely honest with me. It seems that,
suddenly, everyone wanted to be terribly loyal
and honest. Infuriating! "I feel obliged by the
respect I feel for you to tell you everything. So
you'll know this isn't just some passing fancy.
This time—and I regret it as much as you do—it's
serious."

I regret it as much as you do…well, I never.
But he said it in all seriousness. That he regretted
it as much as I did.

But let's return to Lisa's smile, according to
Ernesto Laje. If you could call a smile straight,
it was a straight smile. It moved horizontally

through everything, going exactly where it needed to go. As for her eyes... Well, Ernesto spoke at length about them too:

"Imagine a young girl daydreaming in a deserted house. Suddenly I wasn't even there. Her gaze embraced everything, but without seeing anyone, not even me, though I was right there in front of her. As I'd discover later, her gaze has the strange ability to turn people and things into glass or even air, to simply pass right through them and continue on in search of what really interests her. It's as if anyone who fails to capture her attention doesn't exist—and so they don't, she delivers the coup de grâce by making them invisible."

However, that afternoon, before supper, she looked at him and smiled a lot. She also talked, and what she said was just delightful. So full of life, so..."

"So young, given that she's young enough to be your daughter."

He shrugged: "Yes, she is, but fortunately she isn't my daughter."

She, Lisa, Dora Rosário's daughter had said:

"When I think about the things I'll see, the places I'll visit... Me, yes, ME!"

She again opened wide her arms, not in order to fly this time, but to embrace the world. Europe, Asia, Africa, America, and Oceania. "I speak excellent English and German, I'm fit and healthy, so there's no reason why I shouldn't get the job, is there?"

Certainly not with that pale little face and those eyes, like the eyes of an animal who isn't in the least bit frightened (or aggressive), as well as the aforementioned smile, the slender, graceful body, the easy, confident gestures of a dancer—sometimes slow, sometimes fast, but never wrong.

No doubt remembering that such enthusiasm was out of place when her mother, poor thing, was in the hospital and who knows for how long, she returned to earth, or, more precisely, to the third-floor apartment where she lived, and still more precisely to the living room where she was talking to the "owner of the vehicle." She rested her arms on the arms of her chair, her hands hanging limp—small, white, beautifully manicured hands with pink nails.

"My poor mom," she said, for want of anything better to say, and adopted a terribly sad air, which made him long to console her.

"Yes, you're right," he agreed. "Terrible luck. And it's all my fault." (This wasn't true. In his opinion, her "Why?" was still to blame for everything.) "I was driving too fast. It's just fortunate we weren't killed."

"That would have been dreadful," said Lisa.

"It certainly would. Anyway, I came here to offer you any help you might need. Money, anything. I'll leave you my card. You just have to pick up the phone and ask."

"Thank you, but we don't really need anything," she said. "If we had a problem, with money I mean, my grandmother would help us out."

He stood up. "I hope, though, that you'll consider me a friend of the family. There are some things that a grandmother..."

Lisa giggled. "She's not your average grandmother. Of course, she is very old, but...she's a good comrade, though, when needed."

They were at the front door now, and Lisa was holding it open. Ernesto hesitated. "What's your name?" he asked.

"Ana Luísa, but everyone calls me Lisa."

"Lisa Rosário," he said thoughtfully.

"That's right. Lisa Rosário."

"And what if instead of being a stewardess,

Lisa Rosário, you were to travel the world, well, a large part of it, as a passenger at your husband's side."

She giggled again. And because her hair was bothering her, she caught it up on top of her head and fixed it there with a clip she kept in a little pocket in her leggings.

"Definitely not. You sound just like my mother. Young girls now aren't like they were in your day, just sitting around and waiting; no, we know there's almost zero chance of finding love *and* money—it's either one thing or the other. You need to work, of course, but you must choose a job you enjoy. I hate being stuck in the same place all the time. If I were forced to spend my days in the Museum like my mother, I think I'd run away, but before I did I'd smash all that junk to smithereens. I considered becoming a journalist, but is there any proper journalism here? I found my vocation from listening to Aunt Júlia talking about her science-fiction dreams."

"Is this the Aunt Júlia of the flying saucers?" he said, then bit his lip. It was unlikely that Dora Rosário would tell the first client who appeared about family problems or, rather, family secrets.

Lisa frowned slightly but seemed completely unfazed.

"Yes, that's the one. But whereas she just dreams, I'm going to realize my dream. Wanting to do something is important."

"It's the most important part. Without will-power, you're nothing."

Lisa burst out laughing: "You sound like Ana. She's my grandmother."

"Yes, I know."

"Oh, you know that too?" she said rather glumly. "You know a lot of things, don't you?"

For the first time in many years, Ernesto Laje felt rather uncomfortable, and hastened to dispel any suspicion on her part... As gently as he could.

"I had hardly slept the previous night, so I asked your mother to tell me about her life to keep me awake. She very kindly obliged and told me all sorts of things."

"That's not like my mother at all."

He was about to say: "I know," but stopped himself in time. "Well, that only makes her still more deserving of praise," he said instead. "She talked about you, about your grandmother, about Aunt Júlia, and about your father of course. But I just got sleepier and sleepier, and I thought it had all gone in one ear and out the other."

"It must have lodged in your subconscious," declared Lisa with a scholarly air.

"Yes, it must have." He hesitated, then held out his hand. "Anyway, if you don't mind, I'll pop in tomorrow to hear any news of your mother."

"But…" She looked slightly perplexed. "You do know where she is, don't you?"

"Yes, but I thought it best not to bother her. I think only close family members should be allowed to visit."

"Possibly," she said. Then added: "I'm always here around this time. I go straight from my ballet lesson to visit Mom before supper. She doesn't want me to sleep there; she says it's not necessary."

"Do you go dressed like that?" Ernesto asked with genuine curiosity.

"Yes. With a jacket on top. Is that so very extraordinary?" And she laughed again.

The door was already closed, and Ernesto was going slowly down the stairs accompanied by the echo of her laughter. He was going slowly because his body still hurt, but also because he couldn't stay and didn't want to leave. This was the first time such a thing had happened to him. But she's a child, he was thinking. Lisa, though, didn't have the body, the eyes, or the laugh of a child. She was a young girl waiting for love. Unfortunately. Yes, but what was it she had said about money?

The following day, he returned at the same time. Before that, a huge, lavish box of chocolates had been delivered. As soon as he arrived, Lisa rushed to meet him: "They were delicious, I mean, they *are* delicious." She didn't say, "You-really-shouldn't-have," and that pleased Ernesto Laje. Lisa wasn't wearing a leotard this time, but a pleated skirt and a sweater, like any other schoolgirl. She also had a ribbon in her hair. She spoke about her mother, said she was slightly better, and that they might take her stitches out on Saturday; then she asked if he wanted a drink. "There's not much choice," she said, crouching down by a liquor cabinet. "My mother never drinks, and we don't have many visitors." Ernesto accepted a glass of port (which he had always hated) and began, quite naturally, talking about himself. The port wine reminded him of his youth. He hadn't had much money *in those days*, and a glass of port was a big expense. He talked about his friends and the café where they used to meet up. He was working in a shop then and studying at night. And he returned to their conversation from the previous evening: "You said yesterday how important it is to want something, Lisa. And there's really nothing more important. That's how I got my law degree, began to get known as a lawyer, and acquired a broad clientele. I now have an excellent reputation, plenty of money, and have even, more than once, been offered a government post."

"What? As a minister?" she asked, impressed.

"Not quite, but something similar. I've always refused though. Politics ruins people's lives."

"It brings prestige, though, doesn't it?"

"I don't need prestige. Being known is enough. People come from all over the country to consult me…"

He wore the indifferent air of someone who attaches little importance to what he's saying… Of someone who just happened to mention it apropos of…of what exactly?

Oh, that's right, the port wine. "Don't you drink, Lisa?"

"No, it's bad for the figure. I'm terrified of getting fat like Ana, who was already fat by the time she was twenty-five."

She paused for a moment, then said: "My poor mother's going to be left with a big scar on her face."

Ernesto groaned. "Oh, how awful. She'll never forgive me."

"My mother's never put much stock in her physical appearance, although lately…" She looked at him hard. Her gaze no longer had that strange property of turning those she looked at into glass or air; on the contrary, when it touched him, it made him feel more alive—it was almost discomfiting. Ernesto Laje thought Lisa was about to ask him some awkward question. Something like: "What exactly is your relationship with my mother?" or "Do you love each other?" or something along those lines. However, she was merely remembering how her mother had told her that she wasn't considering getting married again, and that there wasn't even anyone she was interested in. And pondering, too, how very strange people of her mother's age were and how unexpected their reactions. No, not unexpected, illogical. If her mother had been telling the truth when she said there was no one she was interested in, then Lisa felt perfectly safe to admit that this man was both attractive and very interesting.

Her grandmother would often look at her as if weighing up her potential and, satisfied with what she saw, say: "If you do fall in love, Lisa, make sure he's a rich man. Don't just fall in love with any Tom, Dick, or Harry. I'm sure you can do it." Hadn't she herself said something similar to her mother? What if she fell in love, what if she allowed herself to fall a little in love with this rich, prestigious, and still attractive man, because when it comes to age, men and women are completely different. Her mother was already old, but Ernesto Laje was still young. How old could he be?

"How old are you?" she asked.

He started. "Forty-two. An old man, eh?"

She tilted her head pensively to the side. Men really were different from women. He looked much younger, she said. Much younger. "Perhaps being a lawyer keeps you young, Senhor Laje."

"Oh, please, call me Ernesto. And forget about my horrible profession."

"Why horrible?" she said, genuinely surprised. "It's a fine profession. Defending people is a fine profession."

"What about prosecuting them? I'm quite prepared to send people to prison. You get hardened to it, you know. You, for example, would be incapable of walking barefoot over pebbles, but I have no problem trampling over the fallen. I'm used to it. You acquire a thick skin."

Her eyes were fixed on his. Serenely. Like someone thinking so hard she's forgotten she's looking at anything.

"I don't believe anyone is entirely innocent. I don't mean the people you prosecute, but people in general. We all seem guilty to some degree. You're sometimes guilty as well, because of your profession. But you must sometimes defend honest people too, so that makes up for it. Not everyone can say as much."

"Where did you learn all these things, Lisa?"

She laughed: "You sound just like my mother. Where did I learn such things? I really don't know. Perhaps in another life. What do they call those people who believe in..."

He interrupted her: "Theosophists."

"That's it."

"But you don't believe in all that, do you, Lisa?"

She looked very serious and her gaze grew slightly less intense.

"The only thing I believe in is life. I know I'm going to be very happy, and I'll do anything I can to achieve that."

"Anything?" he asked, impressed by her frankness.

"Anything."

The following day, he told me he was leaving me. It was all settled. Who? I thought of Dora for some reason. Perhaps because he had gone to see her at the Museum, and she had seemed different. But I couldn't believe what he said when I asked.

"Is it Dora Rosário?"

"No, her daughter."

"What?" I was utterly astonished. "But she's still a child, I mean, she's only about fifteen…"

"She just turned seventeen."

"Exactly. She's a child."

"No, she's a woman."

"And does this 'woman' love you?"

"I don't know. I haven't said anything about it to her yet."

I was absolutely flabbergasted. Lost for words. And then convinced he was telling the truth. He was leaving me, or, rather, he was breaking

up with me even before he could be certain she
would have him. She. Even if there were no Lisa,
he would still be leaving. He was simultaneously
madly in love and mortally bored. Or perhaps
Lisa's mere presence had been enough to throw
a harsh light on my image as the sterile woman
who had, in some way, made his whole existence
sterile. He would arrive home, give me a peck on
the cheek, drink his usual glass of whisky, then
tell me all about his day in great detail, and so I
thought he really loved and needed me. In fact,
I was merely a convenient body beside him, an
ever-attentive audience always ready to express
unconditional admiration when he told me of
yet another professional triumph. My contented
smile and my hand squeezing his were, after
all, a form of homely applause and encourage-
ment. He also received such silent applause in
the courtroom, and even from members of the
public, who, if he passed them in the corridor,
would murmur: "He's amazing that Ernesto Laje,
who would have thought he'd get that man off?"
And still more often: "Who would have thought
that poor man would have been left without a
penny to his name?" It wasn't enough, though,
he needed that applause at home as well, in order

to feel he was lord of a little tailor-made world all his own. It wasn't just that I provided a serene backdrop to his life. No, the reason our relationship had lasted so long was because I provided him with a loyal audience, always ready to give him the unconditional applause he needed. He was, above all, an actor. He didn't really care about the people he defended or prosecuted. He was an actor and wanted applause. Now, however, that forty-two-year-old actor had fallen for the play's ingénue, who was not perhaps a very ingenuous ingénue. It was strange. I had sometimes thought of myself as a bad actress with no real dramatic skill, but I had never thought of him as the actor and me as the audience before. Oh well, there was nothing to be done about it.

"Oh well, there's nothing to be done about it," I said out loud, as casually as I could.

"No, I'm afraid not. It's been really wonderful, but…"

"Please, spare me your kind words. I've heard it all before."

"And was that so very bad?"

"Whether it was or not is irrelevant. It's just that I don't want to hear them now. You have the rest of your life to repeat them to a new audience, who hasn't yet gotten used to them. But *will* you have the rest of your life? I'm not so sure. Twenty-four years is a pretty big age difference, dear Ernesto. Too big."

"Maybe."

"It's lucky we didn't get married… That makes everything much simpler. She doesn't even have to know I exist, does she?"

"Oh, I intend on telling her about you."

"You are loyalty personified, my dear. That's very good of you. You will, of course, tell her that we had been growing apart anyway, that I'm a silly, frivolous woman with whom you couldn't share your problems, that… What else, Ernesto? I'm sorry, I'm exaggerating, no, I really am. Forgive me, my dear. Now just go, I need to be alone. I really do need to be alone."

He went and I was indeed alone.

"My mother's going to be allowed out of bed tomorrow for a while, and she'll be home the next day!" Lisa told him as soon as he arrived that afternoon, bearing another box of chocolates. This news forced him to expedite matters. He sat down, looked at her, and asked:

"Lisa, would you marry me?"

She regarded him more with curiosity than surprise. As if she had been expecting this, and couldn't understand why it had taken him so long.

"I'm very young," she said. "I'd like to experience life to the fullest before losing my freedom. In my family, marriages aren't a beginning, they're an end."

"With me, you would always be free, Lisa. Always. And it would be a beginning, not an end. Your life would be your own. Have you thought about the difficulties you'd face if you were to marry a young man just starting out on a career...?"

She broke in: "I know, I know. My mother told me what happened when my father died, and even before that too, I imagine. Not that she's ever complained, because she still considers those the best years of her life."

"I love you, Lisa. I've never felt like this about anyone. This time it's different. I'm crazy about you."

"Goodness!" she said, laughing.

"I mean it, I'm crazy about you. I want to tell you everything, and then you can tell me what you think. I don't want there to be any lies between us, anything hidden." I imagine this was when he told her about me, and no doubt said that we'd been growing apart for some time, that he was unhappy, that I didn't understand him. I can't be sure, of course, but he must have said something along those lines. He told her about his offices on Avenida de Roma, the house in Sintra, all earned with the sweat of his brow (and his vocal cords, I should add), about the stocks he owned, how much he earned each year, on average that is.

"Goodness!" she said again. "What do you do with all that money?"

"I squirrel it away. It's yours to do with as you like. You want to travel? Fine. Buy clothes and jewels? Excellent. It's all yours."

"Goodness, my head's spinning." She then shook her head as if to stop it from spinning, bit her lower lip, and looked away. "I need to think," she said at last, still without raising her eyes. "I really need to think. I don't imagine I'm going to ask my mother or Ana for their advice, because I know they would approve—well, Ana certainly would. I need time alone to think."

"Do you have a boyfriend?"

She shook her head. "No, I never wanted one. I thought that would... Well, I don't really know what I thought now. I really don't know. Would...would you mind leaving me alone to think? Tomorrow we can talk again, is that all right?"

"Of course, Lisa." This was the second time a woman had told him she needed to be left alone. "Can I call you tomorrow morning?"

"Certainly," she said, holding out one small white hand to him. "I'll be home from half past eleven on. I have class until eleven."

They got Dora Rosário out of bed, or tried, despite some resistance on her part, for she sniveled and whined a little, saying she simply couldn't do it. They insisted, though, telling her she had to, and finally they managed to get her on her feet. Dora Rosário (as the nurses forcing her out of bed must have known) was like an empty doll, her legs unsteady, her stomach weak and threatening to rebel at any moment, her right arm feeling as if it had the weight of the world on it. "Don't be afraid," they said. She wasn't afraid. Afraid of what? No, she was drunk and about to topple over. The room was spinning around her or she was spinning like a top. She grabbed ahold of one of the nuns and was helped back into bed. She felt utterly contented then, and would have liked to stay there forever and for them never to bother her again. That was all she wanted, to lie in that bed. That was all she was silently begging for, to be allowed to stay there. "But tomorrow you'll have to get up, get dressed, and go home." They were speaking to her as if to a child. And she was a child, and responded in a babyish voice that, yes, she would do all those things. "And you've got to make yourself pretty, because your daughter's coming to get you at five o'clock." Yes, of course she would make herself pretty. Tomorrow was a long way off. Tomorrow was an eternity away.

Tomorrow, it turned out, was very close, and she was woken early by the night nurse who came to wash her body clean of all ignominy. The nurse's face was round and pink, oozing health, as if made for some promotional video. Had she been chosen to give hope to those who had lost their health? If you keep nice and quiet and eat everything I set before you, you, too, can be like me. Or something like that. The trouble was that no patient could hope to be like her, because the pictures accompanying the adver-tisement were too good to be true. Before and after using cream X or washing your face with soap Y. The nurse handed her a mirror, combed her hair, and Dora saw once again (she had

realized this the day before) that she was a new
Dora Rosário—again—not the Dora Rosário of
the late-night conversation with her mother-
in-law, nor the Dora she had become following
that conversation, but another. Not voluntarily
antiquated-looking, but involuntarily older. Part
of her face was still covered by a bandage. And
what lay beneath?

"What will that look like, Miss Gomes?"
(That was what the nurse was named: Miss
Gomes.)

The latter responded imperturbably: "Oh,
over time you won't even notice it."

"Over time, eh?" Dora said, smiling wanly.
"I don't have that much time left."

"Don't say that. You're still young!" said
the nurse earnestly, because she was a good
employee.

Dora Rosário, however, did not hear her.
She was studying her face with almost scientific
rigor. It was as if she were making a deep, com-
parative study of what she was seeing now versus
what she had seen two weeks earlier. The visible
part of her face was more flaccid, a series of fine
new lines had appeared, a few crow's feet fanned
out from the corner of her right eye (the other

eye being half-hidden), appearing and disappearing when she tried to smile.

"Do you think cream X...?" she asked the nurse, then shook her head. "Forgive me, I'm talking nonsense. I bet you've never used cream X, have you?"

"No, I've never used any cream, just some cleansing milk at night, before I go to bed. To clean the pores, you understand."

"Of course."

They sat her down in one corner of the sofa, but half an hour later she rang the bell and asked to be allowed to lie on the bed again. When would she be able to return to the Museum, which had been closed for two weeks "due to illness"? When would she be herself again? Would she ever be herself again? When would she see Ernesto Laje again? Would she see him again? After all, there was no reason why she should. He had bought the rug; she had given him her advice. Problem solved. And what about her face? Ah, her face. In Miss Gomes's informed opinion, over time she wouldn't even notice the scar.

Sister Chagas came to see her in the afternoon and seemed very excited: "Well, aren't we looking well?" she said, as if Dora Rosário had just been born or were some particularly precious object. As if a bright future awaited her.

"My daughter will pay you when she comes to get me," she said. "Could you prepare my bill, Sister?"

"It's already been paid!" exclaimed the sister. "The gentleman who was driving the car dropped by this morning at nine o'clock. He even gave us some money for the poor. Your daughter has been keeping him informed."

"Lisa? But I didn't know... Right, in that case..." She automatically touched the bandage covering her face. "Right," she said again. "In that case, it's just a matter of waiting for Lisa and then leaving."

"I bet you won't even miss us..." And Sister Chagas once more seemed to be addressing a small child who had been up to mischief or was about to get up to mischief. ...*you little scamp!* Dora Rosário thought, because "you little scamp" seemed implicit in that pause, as did: "Or you'll feel the back of my hand." She felt suddenly tired, almost exhausted. She closed her eyes then and fell asleep.

*

When she woke, Lisa was there, sitting on the edge of the bed, looking at her. She seemed deep in thought, almost obsessively so. Dora wondered if it had been Lisa's gaze that had woken her, but no. Lisa was clearly looking at her without seeing her. The famous gaze that could turn people into air.

"How long have you been there?" Dora asked.

"I don't really know. Quite a while, half an hour maybe, possibly more."

"Why didn't you wake me up?"

"What for?" asked Lisa with a shrug. "You looked so peaceful, so happy. Do you always look like that when you're sleeping?"

"How should I know? I've never seen myself sleeping. I suppose, like everyone else, I must look dead. Happy but dead."

"Does *everyone* sleeping look dead to you?" asked Lisa.

"The ones I love do, yes. Your father, and you... My heart always skips a beat, because it's as if that person might not wake up again, you know?"

"In a way, yes. That must be a handicap, though."

"Why?" cried Dora in amazement, the left side of Dora. "Why should it be a handicap?"

"Loving someone so much."

"One day, you'll understand."

"I do understand, Mom, perhaps not that thing in itself, but what you feel. You say that one day I'll understand…possibly. It's just that everything is so strange, so unexpected, so confusing…"

"What do you mean?"

"In my mind. I can't understand why…"

"Why what?"

"Why I'm going to marry Ernesto Laje. I gave him my answer today. I was sure you'd approve."

At first, Dora just stared at her blankly, dumbstruck. Lisa? Ernesto Laje? *I'm going to marry him*, she had said. *I gave him my answer today. I was sure you'd approve.* Dora couldn't think straight, her thoughts were all over the place, she didn't even know where to start. Ernesto Laje?

"But he's old enough to be your father. You're still a child, Lisa."

That "he's old enough to be your father" rebounded on her. "That man is my lover!" she screamed silently, although her face remained perfectly composed. Could she even call him her "lover"? It had only been one afternoon and wouldn't be repeated, regardless of Lisa. An afternoon that filled her with belated shame. "No, you can't marry him!" she said at last.

"Why not?"

"As I said, he's old enough to be your father. And then there's Manuela, whom he's lived with for many years, and who is more or less his wife."

"But she isn't his wife, Mom. Besides, he explained to me how they'd pretty much drifted apart. And he didn't think of her as his wife. She was just a youthful error, and then he found it impossible to leave her."

"You're about to make another youthful error, Lisa. Ernesto is forty-two. In ten years he'll be an old man and you'll be twenty-seven. One of you is going to end up being very unhappy. Think about it."

"I already have. I thought about it all night. And I *will* be happy."

"Have you spoken to your grandmother?"

"To Ana? No, why should I? She'll be over the moon."

Dora Rosário bowed her head. "Will she? Possibly, yes, she might well be. But I'm your mother, and it's my place to advise you."

"Mom, I love your words of advice. They're

always so sensible, but I'm much more sensible than you. You married a man who was poor and lazy. No, listen, Ana herself told me that my father was lazy and never did anything with his life, never wanted to. I'm going to marry a rich, energetic man who loves me. You've spent years yearning for the good old times, as if they were something to be savored. I'm more sensible. As for the matter of age, we'll see. There's time, lots of time."

"How did all this happen?" asked Dora after a long silence, once she had regained the power of speech.

Lisa shrugged: "He turned up at the apartment to find out how you were. The next day, he sent me a box of chocolates. He's crazy about me. As for me…"

"As for you?"

"I'm beginning to love him, to look for reasons to love him…and finding them too. He's still a good-looking man, despite a few gray hairs. I'll get him to dye them and that will be that. Or I'll simply decide not to see them. He's intelligent. It's good to live with someone intelligent. He's well known. That's another good thing, to have a name that's quite famous in a way. He earns lots of money. I can travel, buy jewelry, fur coats, all those things I never even dared dream of having. Jewelry and fur coats like Madalena's mother. There's Jaime, of course. He's going to be disappointed, poor thing."

"Were you really not even a little in love with him, with Jaime?"

"No, I told you I wasn't. He was too boring."

"That's a shame."

"Is it?"

"Going back to the matter of Manuela."

And she did, as she told me that day. And Lisa listened intently. "A woman who has given her whole life to that man. She was married and left her husband to go and live with him. That's the only reason they didn't get married. And now he's going to leave her because of you."

"He's already left her. Yesterday. Before he even knew what my answer would be. He didn't want me to feel guilty, he wanted to spare me that."

"They might get back together again. He's always loved Manuela. He's had a few brief flings, but he's always gone back to her. She's well into her forties now, and that's her life over. Cut short by you. I really don't like this, Lisa. Call him and tell him you've changed your mind, that it's impossible. Do it today, when we get home. Please, Lisa. You're so young, a child."

"No, I don't think I will call him and tell him that. No, I won't."

The nun came in then with the nurse behind her and asked if they wanted her to call a taxi. Dora Rosário nodded and, with some effort, got up from the bed, while Lisa took her suitcase. The cleaners were all waiting in the corridor to say goodbye and receive their usual tip. Dora Rosário, however, barely noticed them. She was a clockwork toy that had only been wound up enough to make it to the door.

She had just lain down and closed her eyes—ah, the bliss of finding her own bed waiting for her—when her mother-in-law and Aunt Júlia arrived. They immediately sat down and asked for all the details of the accident. They hadn't wanted to ask too much when she was in the hospital, but now that she was better, almost recovered, they were dying of curiosity… Had the car skidded or hit a tree? Dr. Laje was obviously one of those speed maniacs, said her aunt. Her mother-in-law gave a brief speech about irresponsible people putting their own lives and those of others at risk. And since, for her, the word "passing" had an almost demoniacal meaning, she asked: "I suppose he tried to pass someone. That's what they usually do." Then without waiting for an answer, she went on: "The newspapers are full of accidents like that, and most are the result of drivers passing, it's a well-known fact." Then, lowering her voice a little, she asked: "Tell me, doesn't that Dr. Laje fellow live with one of the Lewis daughters, whose family owns the Portofino factories?"

"Yes, he does. She's a friend of mine."

"Oh, I didn't know that."

Ana said this then fell silent, as she often did after speaking, having forgotten what she was talking about. Lost in the wilderness and rather enjoying it. Her eyelids would droop, and her mouth sag slightly, and she'd appear to have passed gently through the door into sleep. Her face then was like a death mask that someone— showing a complete lack of respect—had amused himself by dabbing with red and black, adding a touch of blue on her large, closed lids. She was slipping slowly into senility, almost without realizing it. Aunt Júlia nudged her gently: "Wake up, Ana!" and Ana started awake, then smiled. "I didn't sleep a wink last night, and I'm sleepy, so sleepy. Sorry, Dora, it's not like me at all."

Lisa then placed herself in the middle of the room, curtsied, and said: "Ana, your sleepiness is about to vanish, as surely as my name's Ana Luísa. Your sleepiness will be transformed into enthusiasm, into euphoria. Ana, stand up and let's dance."

"The girl's completely crazy!" said Ana, laughing.

"No, I'm not, you'll see. I'm brimming with common sense. I'm going to do all kinds of things, and while you're still alive too. You'll see, Ana. Loads of things."

"What things, you silly creature?"

"Trips abroad, as many as I want, a house in Lisbon and, for weekend visits, another house up in the hills near Sintra, complete with a swimming pool, plus a few fur coats, real fur, mind, only the best, and jewelry… What do you think of that as a plan?"

"Lisa!" said Dora Rosário, struggling to sit up in bed. "Please, be quiet. Remember what I told you."

"Oh, Mom, you didn't tell me anything I didn't know already."

And when Ana asked what was going on, because she didn't understand a thing, Lisa laughed out loud and again began to dance.

"Stop it!" Dora Rosário screamed, making as if to cover her ears with her hands. Her eyes were unnaturally bright. "Stop it!" And then: "Go away, I want to be alone. Just go, all of you, I want to be alone, *alone*, do you hear?"

This was completely unprecedented behavior. Her mother-in-law left at once, bearing her flabby belly before her. "She must have had a blow to the head," she was muttering. "But you really were being very irritating, Lisa. What did you mean by all this nonsense?"

"I'm going to be married, Ana."

"You?" roared her grandmother.

"To Ernesto Laje."

Her grandmother fell silent, thinking.

"But he lives..." she began saying in a low voice.

"Not anymore. He used to."

"Ah!"

Another silence during which she closed her eyes, so that her face looked even more mask-like. "I think you're doing the right thing," she said at last. "Let me give you a kiss, because you deserve it."

I'm imagining this scene, which Dora Rosário didn't describe to me because she wasn't there. She had stayed in her room, metaphorically covering her ears with her one good hand. I want to be alone, she had said. So many people wanting to be alone.

Her daughter had been married almost a year, after a lavish ceremony in the Basílica da Estrela (a recently acquired dream of Lisa's), when Dora Rosário called and asked if she could come to my house. She needed to see me urgently. I said, "Yes, of course," and she turned up at the two-room apartment with kitchen and bathroom where I currently live. The Dora who came to clear her name and—insofar as it was possible—her daughter's name, was a very different Dora Rosário from the Salvation Army Dora or the Dora-who-still-had-a-future who had followed almost seamlessly after that. Her face was disfigured by the scar that ran diagonally from her forehead to halfway down her cheek, and she had lost the put-together air that had followed the late-night conversation with her mother-in-law. This was a Dora who wore short skirts and makeup (applied hastily and almost with-out looking in the mirror because what she saw there was too upsetting), but still with traces of the earlier Dora. She once again wore her hair tied back at the nape of her neck, she had runs in her tights, and her shoes were worn down at the heel. Her eyes were either as dull as an empty house or unnaturally bright when she became excited.

"And how about you?" I asked when she had concluded the final chapter of what she had to say.

She shrugged vaguely. "I get by."

"Are you still at the Museum?"

She looked blank. "The owner thought I hadn't been doing a good enough job lately... perhaps I hadn't. There were a few problems, money went missing... Now I work in a fur-niture shop...well, you couldn't even call it that really. I sell basic pinewood furniture, mattresses, sofas."

"You have a wealthy son-in-law."

"I do. His secretary gives me a small pen-sion every month." She blushed scarlet, then said: "Lisa was very insistent that I should go and live with her, but you can imagine... Plus, I've never liked living in other people's houses. And they're always having guests over, suppers, meetings, and now there's a baby on the way…"

"Really?" I said.

"Oh, didn't you know?"

"No, I didn't. Ernesto must be very pleased. He always wanted to have children."

"Yes, I think he is pleased."

She stood up and slowly held out her hand. Then she said with a sigh: "Goodbye, Manuela, and forgive me. I mean…"

She couldn't find quite what it was she meant, and I didn't help her in the search. I opened the door for her and, for some reason, went over to the window to watch her leave. It was raining, and she was a gray woman, slightly bent, lost in a plundered city deserted after the plague. I noticed that she walked uncertainly, hesitantly, teetering slightly, as if she were a little drunk or had not quite woken up from a long sleep.

The rain continued to fall, a gentle, steady, almost slow rain, falling as if reluctantly, passively, from an old and ailing sky, bleary-eyed and weary with life. Now that I lived alone, it was a day like so many others. Another number to be subtracted from my account.

MARIA JUDITE DE CARVALHO (1921–1998) is one of Portugal's most important writers of the second half of the twentieth century. Carvalho's work spans painting, journalism, and fiction, with a specialization in the short story and novella forms. A writer of great concision with an eye on modernization, the changing politics of Portugal, and the effect of contemporary life on everyday people, especially women, Carvalho published widely and to great critical acclaim. *Empty Wardrobes* is her first work available in English.

MARGARET JULL COSTA has worked as a translator for over thirty years, translating the works of many Spanish and Portuguese writers, among them novelists: Javier Marías, José Saramago, and Eça de Queirós, and poets: Fernando Pessoa, Sophia de Mello Breyner Andresen, Mário de Sá-Carneiro, and Ana Luísa Amaral. Her work has brought her many prizes, most recently, the Premio Valle-Inclán for *On the Edge* by Rafael Chirbes. In 2014 she was awarded an OBE for services to literature; and in 2018 she was awarded the Ordem do Infante D. Henrique by the Portuguese government and a Lifetime Achievement Award for Excellence in Translation by the Queen Sofía Spanish Institute, New York.

KATE ZAMBRENO is the author of the novels *O Fallen Angel* (Harper Perennial), *Green Girl* (Harper Perennial), and *Drifts* (Riverhead Books). She is also the author of *Heroines* (Semiotext(e)'s Active Agents), *Book of Mutter* (Semiotexte(e)'s Native Agents), *Appendix Project* (Semiotext(e)'s Native Agents), and *Screen Tests* (Harper Perennial). Columbia University Press published *To Write As If Already Dead*, a study on Hervé Guibert, in June 2021. She is currently at work on an essay collection, *The Missing Person*, and a novel, *Ghosts*. A 2021 Guggenheim Fellow in Nonfiction, she teaches at Columbia University and Sarah Lawrence College.